MW00941363

CONTRACT: SICKO

Sei Assassin Thriller

Ty Hutchinson

Published by Ty Hutchinson
Copyright © 2015 by Ty Hutchinson
Cover Design: Damonza

Phakamon Parsomploy, Dueanphen Buakham,
Preyanan Sophaphan, and Ly Thanh Huong
Thank you for the inspiring conversations.

CONTRACT: SICKO

Sei Assassin Thriller

Chapter 1

The polished handles of the four-inch throwing knives glistened in the light as I secured the tiny buckles on the leather sheath wrapped around my thigh, careful not to chip my manicured nails. Over the years, I had grown quite fond of the little daggers—small and deadly, much like myself. I never left home without a pair or two on me. You'd be surprised at how often I have a need for them.

I lowered my black cocktail dress, smoothed it over my hips, and adjusted the top over my breasts. The dress was Vera Wang; the daggers were titanium. A single strand of cream-colored Akoya pearls circled my neck, and matching earrings dangled from each earlobe. My black hair was pulled back into an elaborate French braid with tendrils framing my face.

A gold-edged mirror hung above the white marble, dual-vanity counter; three women could tend to their makeup and hair without bumping elbows. Brushed chrome fixtures adorned the integrated sinks, and a few personal amenities in matching canisters sat on the counter: hand soap, lotion, and mouthwash.

Against the far wall sat a single white toilet and a bidet

made from the same marble as the countertops. French impressionist art hung on the walls, and a bouquet of fragrant flowers in a crystal vase occupied a small table. There were no windows, but the dozens of crystal droplets on the mini-chandelier scattered warm light throughout the room. The guest bathroom was on the ground floor of an immaculate villa nestled on the shores of Lake Como in Laglio, Italy.

The sun had dipped below the horizon before my arrival allowing the calm surface of the lake to reflect the silver glimmer of the full moon. This was my first visit to the area, so I had spent time researching the town and its residents. The villas that lined the lakefront read like a Who's Who of Italy's wealthy and influential. Villa Oleandra, George Clooney's personal luxury villa, was two doors down. I read that the mayor of Laglio had declared a fine of up to five hundred euros for anyone who approached Clooney's property. I preferred Brad Pitt.

I hadn't any worry about being fined or escorted from the area, as I had secured one of the coveted invitations to the popular black-tie affair held every fall at Villa Fiore by its owners—the Abbandonato family. The sprawling structure sat on two acres of land and was enclosed by a series of stone walls and wrought-iron gates. It was classic Tuscan architecture, with stone-accented stucco exteriors, terracotta roof tiles, rustic wooden shutters and doors with iron ring pulls, two enclosed courtyards, and not one but two observation towers.

Every year, the Abbandonatos held a charity fundraiser, La Buona Volonta Gala, the goodwill affair, and it always raised an incredibly indulgent amount of money. The Children's Charity in Milan was the lucky recipient of this generosity. The charity provided the basics—food, shelter, and clothing—but its passion, its priority, was to instill music into the children's educational development.

Aside from the charitable aspect, the event had long been revered for its delectable dining options. Robert Bertolini, owner and head chef of the Michelin-starred DaVinci, had the honor of preparing the evening's feast. Great pains were always taken to ensure the secrecy of the menu until the removal of the silver cloches covering each course. In the past, guests dined on dishes consisting of fresh Maine lobster, Matsusaka wagyu filets, and whole white truffles from Alba, Italy.

Outside of the gluttonous reasons to attend, the gala gave attendees, a long list of Italy's affluent, an opportunity to rub shoulders with others cut from the same cloth, plan one-of-a-kind holidays, and of course, forge relationships that would lead to lucrative business deals.

Every year, one hundred invitations were hand-delivered to their recipients, who always promptly RSVP'd shortly after. While the invitation allowed entry, it also required a donation of two hundred fifty thousand euros and highly encouraged guests to take part in the silent auction where bids often ran into the millions. So not only did a person have to *be* somebody to receive this honor, it required his or her pockets to be deep and generous. One look at the invitation and it was easy to see that this gala would be nothing but spectacular and worthy of attendance.

That year, the invitations were handcrafted by an artist who specialized in the elaborate and incredibly detailed art of Chinese paper cutting. Opening the invitation revealed a magnificent pop-up scene of the mountains surrounding Lake Como with Villa Fiore front and center. In the past, it wasn't uncommon to find a few of the invitations for sale on eBay for upwards of two thousand euros. I suspected this particular invitation would be no different.

I popped my lips after applying my ruby red lipstick and dabbed Chanel on each wrist. Before leaving the bathroom, I took one last look at a photo before tucking it back inside my clutch. I drew a deep breath and let it pass through puckered lips. Time to locate my mark.

Chapter 2

I exited the bathroom and followed a short hall leading to a large courtyard. The night was cool, even with the portable space heaters fighting the chilly air off the lake. I took a deep breath. The air had a sweet woodsy smell thanks to the fire pit in the middle of the courtyard burning cherry wood. Guests stood in small conversational groups of three to four while sipping champagne from crystal flutes. A few seconds was all I needed to ascertain that every Italian and Parisian designer was well represented. The jewelry adorning the necklines and wrists of the women sparkled enough to total into the millions. A promising haul for someone with that in mind, but I wasn't there to steal jewels.

As I continued to take in the sea of wealth, I couldn't help but feel slightly out of place. While I too had a bank account hosted in Switzerland like many of the attendees, I was sure my coffers didn't come close to matching their holdings. It didn't matter; I wasn't a fan of banks, and I always kept a large stash of cash reserves on or near me. I moved around too much and ATMs pinpointed my location—a liability in my profession.

Although my balance sheet probably couldn't begin to compare with the aristocracy, that night I certainly looked the part. My employer had paid the required donation and covered all the expenses needed to attend the gala: hair, makeup, clothing, and travel. It was a considerable amount, but necessary for me to blend. I could only imagine the costs for those who came with plus twos and threes. I came alone, but I liked it that way since I worked alone. I also despised unnecessary small talk.

It didn't take long for me to spot the man in the photo: Matteo Abbandonato, the CEO of Abbandonato Italian Marble. I had learned earlier that his family was purveyors of Carrara marble, the world's most expensive and sought after. The company was established in 1942 and quickly become well respected in the marble industry thanks to the development of a number of profitable quarries throughout northern Italy. His father, Enzo, had relinquished the daily duties of running the company almost seven years ago. He remained on as chairman, but from my understanding, he was largely a figurehead and wasn't involved in the day-to-day decisions involving the business.

Why so many people attended was mind boggling to me. The lake views were stunning, so I could understand the attraction from a touristic perspective, but these people weren't here on a ten-day tour of the region. I highly doubted the Abbandonatos' guests were genuine friends. I suspected attendance had more to do with puffing out one's chest and gloating about the latest moneymaking scheme rather than catching up.

As I slowly wove my way through the fake laughter and overzealous smiles, a tinge of nausea bubbled in my stomach, but I pushed through and managed a smile of my own.

Matteo stood off to the side of one of the three bars, surrounded by four other men. The looks on their faces told me they weren't discussing their next golf outing but most likely plotting the demise of their competitors. The wealthy retained their wealth because they did whatever it took to continue acquiring it.

As soon as I popped out from behind a gaggle of frosted blondes with enhanced chests, Matteo's eyes fell upon me, resulting in a double take and a hint of a smile. As I neared the bar, he excused himself from his circle and intercepted me.

"Hello. Would you like a drink?" he asked with an Italian accent.

"That would be nice."

He spoke in his native language to the bartender and a few seconds later handed me a champagne flute. "Tonight we're pouring Dom Perignon from 2003. I hope you'll find this particular vintage satisfactory, Ms...."

"De Snajier. Valarie De Snajier."

His left eye squinted in question.

"My father's Dutch and my mother's Chinese," I

followed up.

Matteo's relaxed his face and smiled. "You have a unique look."

I brought the glass to my lips but blocked the flow of bubbly into my mouth with the tip of my tongue.

"How is it?" Matteo motioned with the flute he held.

"Delicious."

Matteo took a sip from his glass before speaking. "Is this your first attendance at La Buona Volontà? I don't believe I've seen you before."

"It is, and thank you for the invitation."

"Of course." Matteo had hazel-colored eyes, a chiseled jawline, a flawless olive complexion, and amazing hair. He stood tall, approximately six-foot-one. I knew from my research that he trained daily in mixed martial arts. Even in a tuxedo his physique stood out.

"Do you personally know all of your guests?"

"Mostly. It's good business."

"Is it always business with you?"

"Depends on the company I share." His smile widened.

"Mr. Abbandonato, you strike me as a man who always gets what he wants."

"Please, call me Matteo. And yes, when something or *someone* gains my attention, that's usually the case."

I pretended to take another sip while I looked around. "You have a beautiful home."

"It's been in my family for three generations." Matteo

grabbed another glass of champagne and then offered me his arm. "Come, I'll give you a personal tour."

I smiled. *Perfect.*

Chapter 3

Matteo escorted me around the bar and past a row of large balled topiaries in boxwood planters adorned with decorative pewter lion-head knockers.

"We'll escape through here. The other way will have me stopping and chatting with every guest I pass."

"I feel special."

Matteo glanced my way. "I have that effect on women."

"Are you always so arrogant?" I said with a forced laugh as I kept in step.

"I call it confidence."

"Semantics."

"Are you always so guarded?"

"That might be disinterest that you're sensing," I said with a coy smile.

"Feisty. I like it."

Matteo pushed open a pair of French doors leading into a small sitting room. The lights were off, but enough moonlight shone through the doors and windows allowing us to move easily around the furniture.

We exited the room and entered a long hallway. Two

things caught my attention immediately: the hand-carved wainscoting made from wood and the painted portraits that hung along the left side of the terracotta-colored wall. The portraits, all of them, were of men and each one accompanied by its own display lighting.

"Family?" I inquired.

"Yes. That's my father, my grandfather, and the tenacious-looking one at the far end is my great-grandfather, Corrado Giovanni," he said, pointing.

"Giovanni?"

"Yes, my family is Sicilian. My great-grandfather changed his last name when he started the company. He felt there was a stigma attached to Sicilians."

"It appears that it worked in his favor," I said, running my fingers gently along the wall.

Matteo nodded. "He had no money, no education, but an intense desire to succeed. Abbandonato Italian Marble exists only because of him."

"Where are the women?" I asked as I perused the portraits.

"There's another hallway reserved for the matriarchs of the family."

"I don't see your picture?"

"One will be commissioned when I marry. That's the tradition."

"Well, you better hurry before you end up with a portrait that makes you look older than Corrado."

Matteo laughed. "Come on. Let me show you the grand library." We walked to the end of the hall, through another sitting room, and into another smaller hall with similar architectural accents as the first one we'd passed through. "You'll like this," he said as he put effort into pushing open two wooden doors.

"Grand" was an understatement. That familiar musty-library smell flooded my nostrils as my eyes took in the scene. Hundreds of hardbound books lined towering built-in bookshelves.

"There are over ten thousand books in here," Matteo said as he stood by my side. "The first floor houses the classics and favorites of the family. The second floor is all Italian, mostly first editions."

A wooden staircase spiraled from the first to the second floor. Its deep red color reminded me of a glass of cabernet. The newel at the end of the left handrail was an impeccably detailed lion's head. I could practically hear it roaring.

"We spared no expense when it came to building the library," Matteo said as he ran a hand over the lion's head. "The shelving, the staircase, the floor, the furniture, all of it custom-built from solid East Indian rosewood."

"Do you spend much time in here?"

"When I was child, it was my favorite room in the house. I would spend hours reading on that chair until I fell asleep."

I walked over to an enormous wooden globe—the

diameter had to be about four feet. Each continent had impressive detailing like a 3-D topographical map. The Himalayas, the Andes, the Rockies—all the great mountain ranges were visible to the eye. Even the currents in the oceans stood out.

"It was hand carved and painted by an artist in Florence. It's a one of a kind."

"Impressive," I said, spinning it slowly.

"Come, there's more to see."

During our walk, I learned that Matteo had moved back into the villa just two years earlier. His only sister lived in Paris and his mother passed away five years ago from breast cancer. Since her passing, his father had found new love and moved to the south of Italy for the warmer weather. The villa stood empty for almost a year before Matteo returned to Lake Como. "I was hesitant. I enjoyed my life in Milan."

"You enjoyed the fashion models there."

He laughed. "You could say that."

"Tell me, why at your age are you not already married? I think I read somewhere that you're one of Italy's most eligible bachelors."

"First, I'm only thirty-four—hardly an old man. Second, do you always believe everything you read?"

"So does the bachelor maintain a proper office or one of those childish man caves?"

Matteo led me to a door with a password protected electronic lock. He punched the code into the keypad and then pushed open the wooden door. "Does this answer your question?" he asked, gesturing.

The spacious office had a nautical décor. Hanging on the walls were framed hand-drawn charts, a shadow box containing an array of navigational tools, and a brass anchor. Behind a cherry wood desk stood an impressive display case holding a wooden scale model of what appeared to be a Spanish galleon. Matching bookcases were built into three of the four walls. Books and more nautical knick-knacks lined them. Opposite the desk were two brown leather armchairs and a matching sofa. A glass coffee table with a fresh floral arrangement sat between them. French doors led to a private balcony.

"No need for any lights," he said. "I'm not a fan."

"I agree. The moonlight's enough."

"There's a wonderful view of the lake from the balcony."

He took my empty glass—I had emptied my champagne into a potted plant along the tour—and placed it with his on the desk. A pad, a pen, and a laptop were the only items on it.

Matteo had been right about the view. We were on the second floor of the villa and had unobstructed views of the lake and its silvery reflection of the moon. I wasn't quite sure where we were in the villa in relation to the gala, but it was quiet, save for the faint singing of crickets and a slight rustling in the lemon trees below.

I must have had goose pimples on my shoulders because Matteo draped his jacket around my shoulders.

"Better?" he asked as he stood behind me. Not waiting for an answer, he wrapped both arms around me. I didn't push away, and it didn't take long before I felt his lips gently nipping at my neck. I tilted my head to the side and breathed deeply. He wore a woodsy-scented cologne. It was masculine, but not overpowering like some designer ones could be. A soft moan unexpectedly escaped my lips and Matteo saw that as a sign to turn me around.

He grabbed my behind and lifted me up as I simultaneously wrapped both of my legs around his waist. At that point, I sort of expected his tongue to invade my mouth with quick prodding and heavy suction, but it was pleasant. Perfect. Dangerous.

I cupped my hands around his face and increased the intensity of my kisses as he carried me back into the office. He was still walking backward when I slammed my balled fists against his ears, bursting his eardrums and causing extreme pain. I followed with a head butt, connecting in the area above the bridge of his nose, and he released his grasp around me.

I dropped to the ground, and he dropped to a knee. I clasped my hands around the back of his head and forced it down into my knee. His legs gave way, causing him to fall forward onto his hands. I jumped onto his back and hooked an arm under his chin, tightening my arm against his windpipe. He fought it for a few seconds but eventually collapsed to the floor unconscious. I wasn't there to kill him.

Chapter 4

Retrieving my clutch from the balcony railing, I removed a memory stick and a pair of latex gloves and hurried over to the desk. I snapped the gloves on and then jabbed my finger at the space bar on the laptop, prompting the dark screen to glow bright and the laptop's innards to churn to life. I stuck the stick into the USB port and proceeded to download the contents of the hard drive. My employer, the CIA, had informed me prior to the start of my mission that the laptop was kept in a secured office—one that only Matteo had the code to enter. I had no idea what the CIA wanted with the information on Matteo's laptop, but it must have been important enough for them to use me to get it.

While waiting, my curiosity grew and I poked around on the computer's desktop. I didn't see anything incriminating. I opened a few folders and saw the usual documents one would expect to find on a businessman's laptop: invoices, spreadsheets, sales reports, and contracts. I clicked on Matteo's inbox and skimmed his emails. Most had to do with the business of his company. There were a few personal emails from women, girlfriends, I suspected.

Maybe what the CIA wanted had been buried deep in a systems folder. Whatever they were looking for, it wasn't obvious.

It was unusual for the CIA to use me for something like this. The job wasn't high risk, and I highly doubted that if something were to go wrong, it could be traced back to them. Political fallout wasn't a worry. A scandal perhaps, but that was about it.

The CIA could have easily inserted one of their own with the skills necessary to seduce Matteo. The security around the villa, while noticeable, was nothing more than a generic security firm hired specifically for the party. Men were stationed mostly around the perimeter, primarily to keep uninvited guests from entering, not to keep out someone like me. They were armed, but it was not as if they were protecting dignitaries. I noticed no video surveillance during the tour and aside from his office, Matteo never turned on or off an alarm or unlocked a room. Any decent thief could have gained entrance to the villa and probably figured out a way into his office.

The other odd thing about the assignment were the two directives given me: "No one dies," and "Make it look like a theft from a competitor of Abbandonato Italian Marble." A sexy siren was sent to seduce the CEO and steal company secrets. Seemed completely believable.

I glanced at Matteo; he was still unconscious. I had less than a minute left on the file transfer and hoped he wouldn't recover before then. I'd had the element of surprise on my side, which had made it very easy to put him down. With his MMA training, it would have been a different fight had he known I was a threat.

I walked over to where his jacket had fallen off of me and slipped a business card into the pocket. The CIA had gone through great lengths to create a believable background, starting with my alias, Valerie De Snajier. Sei the assassin wasn't apropos. The title on the card stated that I was a consultant for Agro Industries, a consulting firm for the mining industry in Luxembourg. There was a phone number and a web address that led to a dummy website the CIA had built, which touted the firm's expertise in semi-precious and precious stones as well as marble. The CIA wanted to ensure that this came across as nothing more than one company stealing secrets from another. Emails were answered; even phone calls reached a live person.

The laptop dinged, and I retrieved the memory stick, tucking it safely into my clutch before wiping my prints off of my champagne flute. I had done everything the CIA instructed me to do. The only thing left to do was to leave.

But that would have been too perfect, now wouldn't it?

Chapter 5

As I headed toward the door, a hand gripped my ankle and yanked my leg back. Matteo had caught me off guard and caused me to almost fall forward onto the floor. *Damn heels.* I used both arms to steady myself, but I still fell to one knee. I quickly shook my leg free, got back to my feet, and kicked off my heels. Matteo had already risen by then—all six feet one inch of him.

"I should have known," he snarled.

He stood slightly hunched with his arms dangling in front of him. Swelling had formed near the insides of his eyes, and his labored breathing was noticeable. It was possible that I had fractured his nose, though I hadn't heard a crunch when I struck him, and I saw no blood.

No sooner had he spoken than he charged with balled fists. I backed up while using my arms and head movements to avoid the blows, allowing only one lucky swing to graze the side of my head. My forearms took the brunt of the beating. Matteo had incredible strength, and a direct hit would be punishing. To keep the distance, I used a series of straight kicks to his midsection, alternating with kicks to his outer thigh. His legs were meaty and toned, but still, a person could only take so many hits before his leg buckled from the bruising pain. I backed around the leather sofa.

"You can't escape. There are guards all over this place. One phone call and they'll lock down the property."

"But you won't do that. It would be a declaration of defeat. The great Matteo Abbandonato was unable to defend himself against a woman half his size. You'll be the laughingstock, and people will question the good of all that training in the gym."

Matteo dove over the sofa toward me. I shifted my body to the side just in time to miss a tackle. He hit the floor and tumbled backward then up to his feet. With his back still toward me, I delivered two leg kicks to his right hamstring. His right leg buckled and sent him down to one knee.

I moved in with a flying knee to the side of his head, snapping it to the side. He dropped to all fours and tried to shake off the effects of the blow. I took advantage of the moment and jumped onto his back, attempting the same chokehold that had rendered him unconscious earlier, but Matteo defended against it by tucking in his chin. I couldn't quite get my forearm hooked under it to restrict the blood flow. I kept trying, and that was my mistake.

He stood up with me still clinging to his back, with my legs wrapped around his waist, as I fought to apply the chokehold. I cursed the order that no one should die. It would have been so much easier, and this mess would have been avoided. The longer the fight continued, the greater the chance I could lose or someone would eventually hear the noise.

A drawn-out fistfight wasn't ideal. He was stronger, outweighed me, and had enough training to be a formidable opponent. While confident with my own abilities, I wasn't one to take a chance. In my profession, staying alive was guided by two principles: make it deadly and do it quickly.

I kicked my right heel back into Matteo's gut, hoping to connect with his groin, but my leg wasn't long enough. I repeated the foot blows to wear him down. He swung from side to side, hoping to buck me off, but I clung like a stubborn barnacle. He backed up quickly, slamming me into the wall, forcing my breath from me and sending a sharp pain down my spine.

Matteo threw his head back repeatedly, but I had my cheek pressed tightly against his, moving in sync to avoid his attempt at a head butt. The fight dragged on, increasing the odds of alerting his security. If that were to happen, my no-kill directive would certainly fall to the side. I bit down on his earlobe, hoping to end our stalemate.

"You bitch!"

I spit a chunk of flesh from my mouth.

In a desperate attempt to shake me off, Matteo twisted with a jerk. Surely he would think to fall back and use me as cushioning. I released my arms from his neck and slammed my fists into his ears again, stunning him briefly. I jumped off his back and swung my right leg around, kicking his legs out from under him. He fell onto his side but rolled over and up onto all fours. As he began to stand, I punted my foot into his ribcage and he folded.

I grabbed a handful of hair, steadied his head, and delivered a series of knee strikes to his face, but Matteo was still able to wrap his arms around my thighs and drive me back onto the floor. He was seconds away from mounting me and pinning my arms with his knees, leaving my face unguarded. I couldn't allow that to happen.

I reached down to my right thigh for one of the small knives but all I felt was the sheath. Matteo had his right leg along my left side and scooted up. My guard was no match for him. I continued to search for the familiar handle, the one that felt like home in the palm of my hand, but still I couldn't seem to locate it. *The knives couldn't have fallen out. I checked the buckles. I tugged on them. Everything was secure.* Yet, I couldn't locate one.

Matteo slipped his left leg up along my right side. He sat high on my chest. The pressure from his weight made it increasingly hard to breath. With my left hand pinned against the floor, he reached for the other. His hand latched onto my right wrist, but I shook it free. He grasped again and again and until finally locking onto it. I struggled to prevent him from bringing my arm back around my head, but his strength was too much. And just as he started to pull my hand away from my thigh, my fingers rested on the familiar cold titanium.

Feeling my hands around the handle of the knife gave me a surge of energy and strength. I ripped the knife out, broke free of Matteo's grip, and delivered repeated blows to the side of his torso. His ribcage deflected the first two strikes, but the others found his fleshy abdomen.

The penetration wasn't deep, but his face winced in pain with each stab. Even so, Matteo showed resilience and latched onto my hand. The combination of his full weight on me and the amount of exertion I had already expended had taken its toll. I felt my grip on the knife weaken. *No! Hang on.*

A second later, the knife was in Matteo's hand.

He raised his arm above his head, the knife firmly in his grip with its pointed tip aimed directly at my face. His eyes were dark and penetrating. His brow furrowed with rage. He had every intention to kill me.

Instinctively I jammed a finger into one of the wounds in his side, hooked it, and forced it in and out. Matteo let out a cry and threw his head back in agony. He dropped his arm and collapsed a bit, babying his side. I reached for the other knife instantly and then drove it upward into his neck.

Chapter 6

The following morning, the Le Frecce high-speed train zipped me from Milan to Rome in two and a half hours, putting me at the Roma Termini train station at seven p.m. I would have taken an earlier train, but the tickets for the high-speed train had sold out and only the slower regional train, which took ten hours, was available. Either way, I wouldn't arrive at my destination until early evening, but sitting cooped up on a train for that long wasn't inviting.

After dispatching Matteo, I stuffed his body under a table in the corner of the office. It would be found, but not without effort. There was blood on a small area rug, which I simply flipped over. The stains weren't as visible on the reverse side. His office had a small bathroom attached, and I was able to quickly clean up. Thankfully my dress wasn't too soiled—nothing warm water and a little soap couldn't take care of.

I was able to slip back downstairs and into the party undetected. It probably had to do with the fact that I wasn't anyone of significant importance and therefore not worthy of an extensive chat, or even a smile and a glance, for that matter. Being a nobody had its advantages that night.

After exiting the train station, I walked over to a bank of taxis waiting for fares. I traveled light, just a small knapsack that fit close to my back. Inside I had a change of clothes, a few personal amenities, a titanium fixed-blade knife, a garrote wire, a Sig Sauer P320 with sound suppression, two extra magazines, and a couple of throwing knives.

My destination was the Borgo Pio neighborhood, an area located just north of Castel Sant'Angelo, the Castle of the Holy Angel. Compared to other parts of Rome, Borgo wasn't a heavily touristic area—mostly apartments of working-class Romans. I had been instructed to meet my CIA contact at a small Italian restaurant.

Wanting to continue on by foot to survey the surrounding area—habit—I had the taxi stop a few blocks away from the location. I had spoken to Kostas Demos, my handler with the CIA, shortly after I left the Abbandonato residence the night before. I kept the conversation brief and informed him that I had the information and would see him the following day. I didn't bother to elaborate beyond that. I wasn't much of a phone person.

I first met Kostas a year ago in Turkey. A job had gone wrong and I'd needed to get out of the country quickly while staying under the radar. My employer had hired Kostas as a driver. At the time, I'd had no idea he worked for the CIA, and neither did my employer. I spent almost a week with a man I found irritating and charming all at once.

When the jig was up on his identity, we came to an exclusive agreement that mutually benefitted us both.

Il Quartiere, The Neighborhood, was the name of the restaurant Kostas chose for our meeting place. It was hidden fifty yards back on a quiet street just off of Viale Giulio Cesare Boulevard. By the time I arrived, it was seven thirty p.m.

The restaurant was quaint, only seven tables, and most likely frequented by only the surrounding residents. The décor inside was charming and played up the neighborhood theme. Strung across the ceiling were clotheslines with laundry drying. The lines were attached to murals on the wall depicting the outside of a residential building: windows up high with doorsteps, mailboxes, and flowerbeds below.

Kostas had chosen a table off to the side near the rear of the restaurant. He was dressed casually, a white button-down tucked into faded blue jeans. The waviness in his brown hair had been trimmed a bit, but it still retained its thickness. As I approached, he stood and reached his hand across the table for two. "You killed him."

"Should you be speaking so openly?" I shook his hand and then removed my knapsack and leather jacket.

"We own this restaurant," he said as he sat. He then poured San Pellegrino into my glass.

I looked around at the empty tables. "Explains the crowd tonight." I removed the memory stick from my knapsack and handed it to him. "It's all there, the entire content of his laptop."

He took it from me and dropped it into the front pocket of his shirt. "Are you going to explain to me why you ignored my directive?"

"I didn't ignore it, but you know this business we're in. Things can go wrong fast."

Kostas shifted in his seat and shook his head. "Sei, you could have given me a heads-up when we spoke last night. I was blindsided by my superiors this morning with the news."

"I did my best to get in and get out. You should know that deadly force was a last resort. It could have been me lying dead on that floor. Did that thought cross your mind?"

Kostas sat there befuddled as he managed a response. "I didn't mean it that way."

"You're a bit cold. What happened to the playful puppy dog who drove me across Turkey?"

"Puppy dog? I would say the attraction was mutual."

"Attraction?" I let out a burst of laughter. "Me avoiding eye contact and ignoring your questions is what you view as signs of attraction?" When we first met, I wasn't as friendly as I could have been but I never was with most people. "With this candle-lit dinner, I suspect you'll want to marry me straight away."

"Be careful what you wish for."

"Back to the topic at hand. Isn't this wrinkle the reason you utilize someone like me, so that if something does go wrong, it won't come back to your agency?"

I watched him swish his lips swish from side to side. His olive complexion was still smooth. His appearance still youthful.

"Look," he said, "I'm glad you got out safely. I would have felt bad if you got hurt or—"

"I did get hurt." I pushed back the sleeve of my thin black sweater, revealing the bruising along my forearm.

He must have warmed up because he kissed two fingers and placed them gently against my arm. "Does that help?" Just then, a server appeared carrying two plates of food.

"I hope you don't mind, I ordered for us. Truffle gnocchi. It's excellent." He flashed a smile that showed off his dimples.

While we ate, I relayed the events of the night to Kostas and why Matteo Abbandonato ended up dead. When I finished, he agreed that I really had done my best to stick to the plan.

"I forgot to ask about your daughter the last time we spoke," he said.

"Yes, you were all business."

Almost a year had passed since I discovered my daughter was alive. Two years before, I was led to believe she had died during childbirth. I even buried a body. Turned out she was kidnapped from the clinic shortly after I gave birth.

"Last I knew you were chasing down a lead by an ex-employer."

"That turned out to be a monumental waste of my time. Three months to be exact."

"Ouch. That's not good." He forked a gnocchi into his mouth. "And other than that?" he asked in between chews.

"Nothing. But to be honest, when I vacated my safe house in Belgium, I left behind a large stockpile of cash and expensive weaponry. I've been working to replenish that inventory. That requires accepting jobs—lots of time and energy. A necessary evil."

"You have a new safe house?"

"I do, and I'm not telling where." I used my fork to cut a gnocchi in half.

"Have you thought of what you will do when you find your daughter?"

"The plan remains as it always has. I'll do my best to give her a normal life, one far from this. It's always what I had intended."

"Is that why you went into your self-imposed exile?"

"Exile? I believe it's referred to as retirement." When I discovered I was pregnant, I cut ties with the father, a fling really, stopped working and bought a nice little cottage in Belgium. Even after giving birth, I remained off the grid, still unsure of what to do with my life. Resuming my work as an assassin was never a consideration until I received news that my daughter was alive.

"For some reason, I find it hard to see you playing house, not that I don't think you're capable of it, it's just that…"

"What?"

"You're so good at what you do," he said with a shrug.

"I appreciate that pat on the back, but the last thing I want is for her to be exposed to this world."

"I think that's the right thing to do. I can become cool Uncle Kostas. The one who always says yes when you say no."

I choked out a laugh before raising my glass.

"What? You don't intend to cut me out of your life, do you, when you find her?"

"Here's to you not having me at your disposal for very long."

We both laughed and clinked glasses. "Speaking of our little arrangement, may I remind you that it's reciprocal? I've seen very little in return on your end."

Working for the CIA, Kostas had access to an unprecedented amount of information and resources. In exchange for my services, he had agreed to help me with the search for my daughter.

He swallowed a bite and then wiped his mouth with a cloth napkin. "Well, today that changes. I have something for you."

He removed his phone from his pants pocket and tapped at the screen. "This is Midou Feki," he said, showing me his picture. "He emigrated from Tunisia to Paris about twelve years ago and since then has worked a number of odd jobs to survive."

"And that's important to me because…?"

"One of those jobs happened to be a security guard at the clinic where you gave birth to your daughter."

My heart nearly punched a hole in my chest. Since learning that my daughter was alive, I hadn't come any closer to determining her whereabouts. The only information I had was that an assassin, the Black Wolf, supposedly had her. And even that wasn't one-hundred-percent confirmed.

"Are you sure? I mean, how do you know?"

I had thought to question the workers at the clinic but the man who arranged the kidnapping provided the staff that day. They weren't actual employees of the clinic but freelancers. To make things worse, Parisian law enforcement had raided the place shortly afterward for fraudulent activity. Someone had tipped off the owner and the employees right before they arrived. They disappeared, as did my opportunity to simply speak to anyone who worked there. The only person I was able to make contact with was Dr. Remy Delacroix—the doctor I had hired to perform the birth.

"How did you find this man?"

"Feki had an ongoing relationship with the Parisian police. Mostly petty crime." Kostas tapped at his phone briefly. "I just emailed you the photo along with his last known address. I can't guarantee that he's still there, but it's a lead."

"Thank you. Thank you very much."

"Good luck, Sei."

Chapter 7

Two days later, I arrived at the Gare du Nord train station in central Paris. My destination was La Cite des 4,000, located about six miles east of the center in La Courneuve. La Cite was a public housing complex erected during the sixties as a social experiment. Like most monolithic complexes of its kind, it did nothing but foster a community that the government promptly turned a blind eye toward for years. The result was a neighborhood full of immigrants, plagued by violent crime and rampant unemployment.

During the eighties, the Parisian government decided on an aggressive plan to fix the problem—its residents would be relocated into smaller and less offensive buildings. For the next two decades, the government demolished sections of La Cite. As far as I knew, only a few of the buildings still remained intact. Midou Feki supposedly lived in one of them.

By the time I reached La Cite, it was nearing nine p.m. There were still three buildings standing, though one of them looked completely vacant and partially demolished, as if the government had changed its mind about twenty minutes into the job. Feki lived in one of the two buildings that stood side by side. The empty building was on the other side of a large grassy field about one hundred yards in length.

On the way to Feki's building, I passed a group of small children kicking a soccer ball back and forth under one of the few working lampposts. Most of the property was poorly lit. No wonder crime continued to flourish. I had the titanium fixed blade tucked into my waistband. The rest of my gear was in the knapsack around my shoulders.

Under the few lamps that did work, I saw that the litter problem went beyond a fast-food container or an empty soda can. I spotted a few old tires, a rusted washing machine, rotting pieces of plywood, and a dead something.

The door leading into Feki's building was slightly bent and angled down from its hinges—the security door secured absolutely nothing. Just inside was the lobby. Off to one side was a counter desk, which was used as a dump for unwanted mail rather than to provide a service. The wall opposite the desk held rows of locked postboxes.

After waiting a few minutes, I determined the elevator wasn't working, so I climbed the stairs to the third floor. I'd hate to be the person living on the twentieth.

Feki's apartment, number 333, was near the end of an empty hallway. Just the scuff of my shoes could be heard on the tiles every now and then. It wasn't until I reached his door that I heard other signs of life—a television blaring from inside. I assumed he still lived here, or least someone did. I knocked and waited. No one answered so I knocked again and called his name—still no answer.

I wasn't feeling terribly patient. I exited the building and scanned the third-floor balconies until I located his apartment at the very end; it was one of the few that had a light emanating from it. I used the other balconies to scale the building, and a few seconds later I climbed over the railing leading to his apartment.

The sight of a strange woman entering his apartment, clad in all black, sent Feki running. I tackled him before he could reach his front door. He wasn't a big man, maybe five-foot-seven with a skinny build—about one hundred forty-five pounds. I quickly maneuvered onto his back, wrapped my legs around his torso, and hooked both of my arms under his armpits, locking my hands behind his head.

"Midou Feki, I'm not here to hurt you." I kept my voice calm.

He struggled for a few more seconds before giving up.

"Who are you?" he asked with an accent.

"I'm not the police. I just want to talk, that's all." I slowly released my hands from his head. "That's it. Just relax."

I unwrapped my legs and then pushed myself up and off of him. "Take a seat on the couch, please."

Surprisingly, he did exactly what I told him. I half expected him to bolt for the front door again. He plopped down on the old couch, his weight causing it to sink into the middle. He kept his hands clasped together on his lap and stared at a pizza box on the small coffee table in front of him. A half-empty bottle of liquor sat next to the box. The cheap particleboard tabletop had a corner missing.

Feki wore a stained blue T-shirt. The ribbed collar was slightly torn. His blue jeans were faded from years of use rather than from a hipster design. My nose made it clear to me that he hadn't showered in days. Dark circles were noticeable under his half-closed eyes, even though his skin tone was darker than the olive complexion most Tunisians had. "Having trouble sleeping?" I asked.

"I've nothing to steal. Look for yourself," he said as he gestured around the room.

He lived in a dingy studio apartment. It had a small kitchen off to the side—a countertop and a sink, with a few hanging cabinets, one missing a door. There was a small bathroom and a closet. A small floor lamp and the television were the only two sources of light. The mismatched furniture all appeared to be acquired third hand. The walls were bare and nothing of value stood out.

"I'm not a thief. I only want to ask you a few questions and then I'll be on my way." I walked over to the television and shut it off. "You worked as a security guard at Clinical Clavel. Do you recall that?"

He nodded slowly before his eyes closed and his head tilted off to the side.

"Feki!" I kicked his leg. "Stay with me." His body jerked, and his eyes shot open. I then proceeded to remind him of the day when masked men showed up to his clinic.

"It was two years ago. Do you remember?"

He squinted as he looked at me. "I remember…you were there, yes?"

"I was. I gave birth to a baby girl that day."

He nodded.

"Those men, they kidnapped my daughter."

Feki raised his hands and shook his head. "I had nothing to do with that."

"What do you know about these men? Did you speak to any of them?"

"I know nothing. I stayed outside in the parking lot."

I rested my hands on my waist and shifted my weight to my left leg. Our conversation was heading nowhere fast. "Think, Feki. Is there anything you can tell me?"

He opened his mouth to speak but stopped.

"What is it? Tell me." I drew my knife to encourage him.

Feki scooted away toward the far edge of the sofa, pulled his legs up to his chest, and held his arms out. "You said you wouldn't hurt me."

"I won't if you tell me everything you know. The decision is yours."

He lowered his legs, and his wide-eyed look receded from his face. "Okay, okay. One of the men I recognized."

"They were wearing masks that day. Did this man remove his?"

He shook his head. "I saw a tattoo on his neck. It looked familiar, but I couldn't remember why until later."

"What was it?" I asked, crinkling my brow.

"He had 'The Bronx' written right here." Feki pointed to the right side of his neck.

"The Bronx? As in New York?"

"No, The Bronx is a nickname given to one of the buildings here by a gang."

I perked up. "Is it the building next door?"

He shook his head. "The government knocked down that building a year ago."

As quickly as hope had risen inside of me, it departed. "Does this man still live here? Do you know his name?"

"I haven't seen him in a long time, maybe three months."

"That's not long. Why was he still here if his building was demolished?"

"I think he had a girlfriend in the building next door."

Before I could ask him for more information, I heard the familiar popping sound made from glass breaking. A split second later, a spray of red erupted from the side of Feki's head.

Chapter 8

I dropped to the floor and slithered on my stomach to a wall. From there I saw a golf ball-sized hole in the sliding glass door leading to the balcony. There was only one direction that shot could have come from—the vacant building across the field.

A sniper? Was that bullet meant for Feki or for me?

That was a question worth asking. Only a foot separated our heads. There was a breeze outside, enough to affect the trajectory of the bullet if it were in fact meant for me. I had enemies.

I looked back at Feki's lifeless body. It was slumped over to the side, and a mess of fluid soaked the sofa's beige fabric. Kostas had said he was nothing more than a petty thief. I couldn't imagine him being threatening enough that someone would want him dead. The shot made the situation even more bizarre. It was over a hundred yards away and under the cover of dark. Even if the shot had gone wide, there was no doubt in my mind it was a professional hit.

Who? Why? If I were the intended target, the obvious and first thought pegged the Abbandonato's as the culprit. Had they somehow discovered my identity? Did they hire someone to come after me? It wasn't hard to imagine that happening. What I found troubling was my second thought. If the family was responsible for hiring a hit man, how did that person track me down so quickly and to this location? Only one other person knew where I was heading.

Could the CIA be behind this?

Was this nothing more than an attempt to tie up loose ends? More importantly, was Kostas involved? That last question troubled me the most. The CIA was fully capable of this behavior. They've been known to issue kill orders for lesser reasons. Still, I found it hard to grasp that I was a threat or that there would be any political fallout on a large scale from Matteo's death that somehow warranted my death. The only hiccup was that I would have expected them to hit me with that shot and not Feki—unless I wasn't the intended target.

Just then another bullet ripped through the glass door. *They're still shooting. Maybe I am the target.* Exiting via the balcony wouldn't work. I would need to use the front door. The only problem: it was directly in front of the balcony and in the sniper's line of fire.

I yanked the electrical cord for the floor lamp out of the socket and the apartment went dark. I crawled to the kitchen, where I stood up just off to the side and lifted myself onto the countertop. Crouching below the row of cabinets, I inched my way toward the curtained window. I moved the flimsy material to the side a few centimeters, enough for me to peek out. I figured the sniper had to be positioned on the fourth or fifth floor and in one of the middle apartments. That would allow him the best view into Feki's place.

A bullet shattered the window, sending a few stinging shards into my cheek. *He's equipped with night vision.* I slipped off the counter back to the floor. It dawned on me that the sniper could simply be pinning me down until another team moved into the apartment. I had to make an attempt through the front door. I needed a distraction, but what?

Chapter 9

It was then I remembered the bottle of liquor on the coffee table. It was in the sniper's line of fire, but I felt I could reach it without much exposure. I made my way over to the table, keeping my body as perpendicular to the floor as possible. The apartment was dark, as was my outfit, but none of that would matter with night vision.

From what I could gauge, only my arm would be vulnerable. I counted to three, reached out, and snatched the bottle. A second later, a bullet splintered the top of the table.

I scooted back toward the kitchen and grabbed a rag off of the countertop, tearing it in half. I stuffed the material into the bottle, making sure the frayed part stuck out of the bottle opening. I tilted the bottle, allowing the cloth to absorb some of the liquid. Satisfied, I searched for the final ingredient to my plan: a match or a lighter.

There were two drawers. One was filled with old silverware, the other a typical junk drawer stuffed with a variety of items ranging from a Phillips screwdriver to unopened mail to pens and pencils to a roll of duct tape. I searched for a minute or so before realizing that Feki had a gas stove.

I turned the knob to the front right burner. The familiar clicking sound rang out and seemed to continue for an eternity before a ring of blue erupted. I remained crouched, leaning forward on the balls of my feet, as I raised the bottle to the burner. Either what I was attempting to do was inventive or idiotic.

The wick of the Molotov cocktail ignited, and a yellowish flame appeared, growing quickly in length. I threw the bottle at the floor directly in front of the balcony. The glass shattered, and a ball of fire erupted. I watched the flames grow taller as they licked at the walls. Almost immediately the curtains succumbed to the yellow devil fueling its appetite. Thick, black smoke billowed upward creating a poisonous ceiling that would fill the entire apartment. Soon a wall of flames sealed off the entrance to the balcony and the sniper's visibility.

I darted for the door just as sniper fire filled the apartment. Bullets tore large holes in the drywall and splintered the cheap wooden door. He was shooting blind, but there was only one way out. I slid to a stop against the door, twisted the knob, and pulled it open.

I stayed low and slipped into the hallway, out of the line of fire. I removed my knife as I stood and looked left and right. I decided against drawing my Sig Sauer just yet. The hall was empty, but that didn't mean I was alone. A few feet down I saw a fire alarm on the wall. I pulled the red handle, and the loud metal ringing of a bell sounded.

Seconds later, a few sprinklers in the hall ceiling spurted to life, while the others dripped. I hoped most of the system in the building worked.

A few residents at far end of the hall stuck their heads out of their doorways. "Get out. Now!" I didn't want to be the cause of any innocent deaths.

I ran to the stairs and stopped on the landing between floors. There were windows leading to a fire escape attached to the back of the building. As much as I wanted to run up and down the halls and pound on all the doors, I couldn't risk staying in the building any longer. I couldn't be sure the sniper was acting alone.

Down the metal stairs of the fire escape I went; other residents in various states of dress and carrying whatever belongings they could joined me. I had to hope that Feki was right when he said the building was mostly empty.

When my feet touched the ground, I made my way along the back of the building. By then I was feeling confident the sniper was alone. That and the fact the residents of the building were filing out allowed me to blend amongst them. I tucked my knife back into my waistband.

By the time I reached the front of the building, a small crowd had poured into the grassy field. They pointed and gawked at the apartment on fire. I looked up at Feki's apartment; it was fully engulfed. Flames beat against the kitchen window. A second later, the glass exploded into pieces.

In the distance I heard sirens. Soon the complex would be milling with people from the fire and police departments. I hurried toward the vacant building, sticking to the far right edge of the field where most of the lampposts weren't working. Broken concrete slabs and pillars from a previous building had been bulldozed into a pile along that area, which provided further coverage. I couldn't be sure the sniper was still in his position searching for me.

The front door to the building was missing, and I ran straight in. I double-stepped it up the stairs, avoiding broken bottles and various building debris. When I reached the fourth floor, I moved slowly down the hall. The smell of urine permeated the air.

Some of the apartments were missing front doors. The few I passed were either empty or contained discarded furniture and belongings from the previous tenants. All of it looked as if it had been picked through.

If this were my contract, I would have positioned myself on either the fourth or fifth floor—most likely the fourth floor. I then would have chosen an apartment that lined up with Feki's—one right in the center of the building. The angle looking into Feki's apartment would have been directly opposite and slightly higher.

I continued down the hall until I reached the apartment in the middle. It still had its front door intact. I pressed my ear gently against the cool wood and listened. *Are you still here?* I heard nothing, so I gripped the handle of my knife tighter and checked the doorknob. It was unlocked.

I pushed open the door and quickly stepped back into the hallway, waiting. I heard no movement—more importantly, no gunfire. I cautiously looked around the doorjamb into the apartment. It was empty, but I knew the sniper had been there. I stepped in. The sliding door to the balcony was open and a table and chair were positioned directly in front, a few feet back. There were bullet casings around the table. I took a seat in the chair. A large chunk of the balcony wall was missing, giving me a clear view of Feki's burning apartment.

Chapter 10

It was near midnight when I returned to my room. Earlier in the day, I had checked into a small B&B on the left bank of the Seine. I wanted to stay away from as many of the tourist attractions as possible, which in Paris was difficult to do.

I was tired and angry, and wanted answers. The attack at Feki's apartment felt a lot like an ambush. Was it? As soon as I left La Cite, I placed a call to Kostas. He never answered, but someone with the CIA always did. The woman answering the phone—it was always a woman—took the ID number assigned to me and a number where I could be reached. Sometimes Kostas would call back right away. Other times it could take hours or even a day. That night it took him two hours.

"Are you okay?" Kostas blurted upon hearing that a sniper had targeted me.

"I'm fine. I'm on the phone with you, aren't I?"

"Start from the beginning. Tell me everything."

With exception of the occasional vocal acknowledgment, Kostas let me speak without interruption—a trait I wished he would demonstrate more often.

"Look, Sei. I don't think the Abbandonato family is behind this. They're not aggressive."

"What's that supposed to mean? It's not as if I assumed his sister had been on the other end of that rifle pulling the trigger."

"What I mean is it's not in the family's nature to retaliate this way. They're Italian, but they're not connected to organized crime."

"If that's so, why is the CIA so interested in them?"

"You know I can't answer that. You'll just have to trust me."

"Okay, what are the odds that a sniper was hired to eliminate Feki?"

Kostas let out a breath. "Good question. I have no idea."

"My point exactly. The sniper put Feki down with his first shot. Contract satisfied. Time to go home. But he didn't. He targeted me."

"So he missed on the first shot?"

"You tell me."

"What do you mean by that?"

I wasn't about to spell it out. Surely the CIA recruited bright individuals to fill their ranks. After a few moments of silence, the light bulb went off.

"Wait. Are you implying that the CIA is behind this?" Kostas asked.

"Who else knew of my location? I would have known if I was being tracked."

"Oh, really? Ninja lady knows all. Sheesh, sometimes you really need to stop drinking your own Kool-Aid."

"My what?"

"Kool-Aid? The powdered drink. Jim Jones? Guyana? Forget it. The CIA had nothing to do with this. It's actually a bit insulting that you would even go there. I mean, I thought we were friends."

"Okay, friend. If this isn't the CIA tying up loose ends in the Abbandonato killing, then what is it? Share your theory, please. And try to be objective. Put yourself in my shoes."

"Look, if the CIA were involved, I would know about it. The Abbandonato mission was mine. In fact, my superiors don't even know who you are. I never reveal the identity of the people I hire. Sure we wish Matteo wasn't dead, but we are not crying over it. We got what we needed. We've already moved on. As for an answer regarding the attack tonight, I haven't a clue. Could it be someone from your past?"

Deep down, I believed Kostas. He had earned my trust long ago. And he was right. I had a lot of enemies. It very well could be someone from my past. I've killed a lot of important and powerful individuals. They were all bastards. Early in my career, I had made a conscious decision to only accept contracts for those who deserved it. These were individuals who contributed no good toward humanity. The world wouldn't miss them. Did that make me a hypocrite, considering my profession? I could see that point being made. I liked to think my employers hired me to dispose of the bad eggs.

"Did Feki offer up any information before he got popped?" Kostas asked.

"Yes, there is a silver lining in all of this."

I told Kostas about the man with the tattoo and how he lived at La Cite. "I don't have a name or a location on him, but his girlfriend still lives there."

"Well, if you can track her down, she might be able to point you toward him. That's hopeful. It would mean Feki's death wasn't in vain."

"It's frustrating. All of my steps forward are tiny at best. Knowing my daughter is alive and somewhere out there...I should be doing more."

"Hey, come on now. You know the drill. Intelligence comes in bits and pieces and it takes time to put together a picture. Don't be so hard on yourself. The important thing to remember is that you're making progress. Don't ever doubt your efforts."

I appreciated what Kostas said. I couldn't remember ever needing a pep talk before, but that night I was glad to hear it.

Chapter 11

The following morning, after waiting for the commuter rush to pass, I arrived at La Cite a little after ten fifteen a.m. I had the taxi driver drop me off at the entry gate and waited until he disappeared around the bend before heading inside. It was a ten-minute walk past patchy fields of dirt and grass and large swaths of desolate concrete before I would reach the two remaining buildings.

A single fluffy cloud defied the weatherman's call for clear skies that day, and the temperature hovered in the mid-sixties Fahrenheit. I wore a black leather jacket, a grey turtleneck, a checkered scarf, jeans, boots, and my knapsack. However, this time, I kept my sheathed knife tucked inside my waistband. I didn't feel threatened by the residents of La Cite. They appeared good-natured and harmless, but after what had happened last night, I didn't want to have to suddenly dig around in my knapsack.

On the way in, I passed a few residents. Some appeared to be heading to a job; others just seemed to be leaving for the day. A few people looked as if they had nowhere in particular to go but just wanted out of their apartments.

When I reached Feki's building, I could clearly see his

fire-ravaged apartment. Both apartments on either side had succumbed to the same fate. Other than that, the fire department had contained the fire to those three units. A man wearing a large parka and a ball cap exited the building, so I assumed there was no major structural damage or surely the authorities would have condemned the building. Or not.

I wondered about Feki's body and what the assessment from law enforcement would be. From the looks of the charred apartment, his body had to be badly burned. Feki's head had still been intact when I left him, but there was a large hole where the bullet exited. Probably didn't need an autopsy to determine that he died from a gunshot wound and not the fire. I thought about it as long as it took for me to walk past his building, and then it became a distant memory.

Two teens were sitting on a low wall near the entrance to the second building. I inquired about the man with the neck tattoo. They shrugged a response, and then continued their conversation. I didn't understand what they were talking about; they were speaking Tunisian, or at least that was what it sounded like. Almost all of the residents had an olive complexion; a few were dark-skinned, but their facial features were definitely Arabic.

I headed inside and up to the second floor, listening for signs for people still at home. If I heard a television, or a baby screaming, anything at all, I knocked. Initially my efforts weren't proving fruitful. The second and third floors were useless. There were twenty floors, but I pushed any negative thoughts from entering my head. I was thankful I did, because on the seventh floor I came across a little boy riding his tricycle in the hallway.

He looked about four years old and seemed to understand English, even though his responses were mostly confined to nodding or shaking his head. I pulled a pen out of my jacket and wrote "The Bronx" on the wall and then pointed at my neck. "Have you seen a man with this tattoo?"

He smiled and nodded.

"Do you know where he lives?"

He nodded again.

I bent down to his level and looked into his light brown eyes. I noticed his left nostril was filled with yellow snot. I cleaned it with a tissue I had tucked in one of my pockets, and the wheezing I had been hearing stopped. "Can you show me?"

He nodded as he got off his tricycle. He grabbed my hand and led me down the hall until we reached apartment 718, where he pointed and smiled. I thanked him.

I was about to knock, but the little boy still stood there, smiling at me. I placed both hands on my thighs and bent down again. "Do you have a name?"

He nodded.

I poked him playfully in his belly, and he squirmed

away.

"My name is Rafik," he said.

"Rafik? That's a wonderful name," I said with a smile.

Rafik tucked his chin down and giggled. He then threw both of his arms around my leg and hugged me tightly. I hugged him back. We didn't speak; we just enjoyed each other's warmth. He wanted to be loved, and I wanted someone to love. I couldn't help but imagine that Rafik was my Mui. I imagined she would hug my leg the same way, squirm the same way, and look at me with the same bright, inquiring eyes.

I wiped my eyes as I watched Rafik run back to his tricycle. I couldn't wait to clean my daughter's nose.

Chapter 12

I didn't hear any noise on the other side of the door, but I remained hopeful. I rapped my knuckles against the thin wood. A few seconds passed before I saw movement in the peephole, then the familiar sounds of two unlatching deadbolts.

The door opened, and a woman in her late twenties peeked at me through the crack. She had green eyes with long lashes, a narrow nose dotted with a few freckles, and short, black hair. From what little I could see, she was still dressed in a light blue nightgown.

"Who are you?" she said with a Tunisian accent.

Her eyelids looked heavy—a sign that she hadn't slept well the night before. Maybe she hadn't with the fire I'd started. I then heard the voice of a young girl screaming playfully in the background followed by another older-sounding girl. They were also speaking English and from the bits and pieces I heard, were arguing over what to watch on the television. Those two could very well be the reason for their mother's sleepless night.

"I'm looking for a man. He has the words 'The Bronx' tattooed on his neck. Do you know him?"

"You didn't answer my question." She shifted her weight from one foot to the other. The yelling continued in the background prompting her to close the door a bit and address the situation. A few seconds later, she turned back to me, her left eyebrow raised. She couldn't be bothered to ask the same question a third time.

"I'm not with the police, but it's important that I find him. Please, will you help me?"

She chewed her bottom lip and exhaled heavily through her nose. "I don't want any trouble."

"I promise, there will be none."

"Everybody promises. You know why? Because it's only words." She let out a dismissive breath. "I have two daughters I must care for. I don't need to invite trouble back into my life."

This woman did her absolute best to put on a strong front, but I saw through it. Her eyes said what her mouth couldn't. Something terrible had happened.

"If I find him, I'll make sure he never comes back here," I said.

Her pursed lips had me wondering what this man had done to make her so hesitant? Had he threatened her life? Clearly her financial situation didn't allow her to leave and disappear. Living here meant he could come back again and again. Add the fact that she also had two young daughters…well, I could understand her not wanting to aggravate her situation.

"What do you want to know?" she asked.

"Let's start with his name."

"Akil Badash." She sniffed before rubbing her nose.

"He's Tunisian?"

She nodded.

"Could you tell me your name?" I figured it couldn't hurt to have Kostas run her name. Something useful might come of it.

"I'm not saying."

"Okay. Do you know where Akil lives or where he works?"

"Work?" She laughed. "I haven't seen him in three months. I don't care where that piece of shit is," she said, rubbing her nose again. "And if you find him, you tell him you didn't talk to me."

"Do you have a picture of him?"

She crinkled her brow and pulled her head back. "Don't you hear me? I don't care about that piece of shit."

"I understand, but I really do need to find him."

She shrugged. "I cannot help you anymore." The door slammed shut in my face, and the deadbolts slid back into place. I wasn't surprised by the abrupt end to our conversation, but I had to wonder if there was more to know and whether I should press harder. For the time being, I was content. I had a name to follow up on. Kostas' lead continued to bear fruit.

Chapter 13

It was eight thirty p.m. in Paris. The night was chilly and the endless drizzle of rain blanketed the entire city. Dr. Remy Delacroix had finished his shift at the Bicetre Hospital and had just arrived at his apartment building. He wore a long, khaki raincoat and hurried toward the awning of an artisanal cheese shop located to the left of the entrance to his building.

Named after its owner, the Fromage Bruno Joubert was a Meilleur Ouvrier de France recipient—the absolute highest honor that the French government could bestow on craftspeople. It wasn't uncommon for people to line up daily to taste Joubert's creations. The most popular was the Roquefort, cut lengthwise and layered with a plum jam.

Delacroix took a moment to look at the display of rounds, triangles, and blocks that filled the shop window. More varieties were kept in the long cooler against the back wall and on display tables covered with straw mats.

Joubert specialized in twenty to thirty varieties of cheeses in his shop. The number depended on the season and his ability to get his hands on certain ingredients. He insisted only on using grass-fed Lacaune sheep milk when the recipe called for it. Delacroix knew him well, as he stopped by the shop once a week to purchase two of Joubert's bestsellers—a Comte that he aged for thirty months and a Camembert that was exceptionally soft and creamy. Joubert always reminded him, "You must store the container upside down when you get home."

Delacroix declared the Camembert the best in Paris. Joubert claimed it was a combination of the unpasteurized cow milk he used and the way he aged the cheese in his shop. That's all he would say about the secret process he developed two decades ago.

Delacroix didn't need to purchase cheese that night. He was simply stalling. While he looked into the shop, his eyes darted to the left, to the right. He yawned as he turned, and again his eyes darted left and right. His right hand was tucked away in his coat pocket, fondling a small canister of pepper spray. He continued the charade of window-shopping until convinced no one had followed him home or was watching him.

There was still a decent amount of foot traffic at that time of night. When a group of men and women passed by, Delacroix followed in step and used them as a way to slip into his building unnoticed.

The long-time doorman of his building, Gaston Tremblay, wasn't at his post when Delacroix entered, which wasn't unusual. Gaston was probably making a delivery to a resident. Delacroix hurried into the manual elevator, slid the gate shut, and pressed the button to his floor.

The elevator jerked and began its climb to the fourth floor. The cool air in the elevator shaft flowed freely through the open cage car, but perspiration still streamed down the sides of his face and neck. He removed a handkerchief and dabbed at the annoyance. Ever since Sei had paid him a visit a year ago, he'd been on edge.

Delacroix walked softly on tile floors, his ears perked for any unusual noises while he checked once more that he had the pepper canister gripped correctly. Before inserting his key into the lock of his front door, he listened carefully for a moment.

Once inside, he put his briefcase down quietly and walked slowly through the foyer, peeking around the corner into an empty living room. He shook his head and chuckled at the absurdity of his actions. *Of course, no one is here. Get a hold of yourself.*

He relaxed, removed his coat, and threw it over a chair. He then headed toward his bedroom. The door was shut, but he couldn't remember if he had closed it before leaving that morning. *One of these days you need to commit to either closing it or leaving it open. There'll be no questioning then.* He approached the door cautiously and pressed his ear lightly against it.

Ding-dong!

Delacroix's entire body jumped at the sound of the doorbell. He shook his head, let out a loud breath, and stomped toward the foyer. Standing on the other side of the peephole was Gaston, the doorman.

"Pardon, Dr. Delacroix, but this envelope was left at the front for you."

"By who?"

"I don't know. I found it sitting on the counter when I returned from a delivery."

Delacroix thanked Gaston and slipped him a few euros before closing and locking the door. He then walked over to his study, retrieved the brass letter opener he kept on his desk, and ripped the top of the envelope open. Inside was a folded piece of legal-pad paper. *What's this?* Delacroix reached for his reading glasses before removing the note. A single word was scribbled on the paper. It read, "Sorry."

And then the floor creaked behind him.

Chapter 14

When I returned to the B&B, I called the service number for Kostas. The line always rang three times before a woman's voice answered.

"Yes."

"My ID number is 1968, and I can be reached at 33-6-56-29-76-32."

Click. Dial tone.

That's how it was with each call. No goodbye. No thank you. No acknowledgement. The protocol certainly didn't confirm or deny who was on the other end. I thought it rude, but I understood. It took Kostas a few minutes to call me.

"Hey, so what's the latest?" He sounded chipper.

"The latest is that I have a name for the tattooed man, but his ex-girlfriend doesn't know where he is. Or so she says. I'm hoping your vast CIA resources can help."

"Sure, but you understand what that means, right?"

"I know. Favor for a favor."

"It's the only way I can give you information without getting in trouble."

"Why? Will your superiors put you in the corner for a

timeout?"

"Come on, Sei. We're helping each other."

"The Abbandonato job has to count for at least three or four favors."

"You ignored one of the directives."

"'Ignore' is a strong word."

"Okay, how about side-stepped?"

"I already explained to you why I did what I did."

"Relax, I'm just playing with you."

"I wish you wouldn't."

"But you're fun."

"I can also be dangerous."

"You wouldn't dare."

"Keep playing if you're curious to find out."

We had a moment of silence as Kostas thought about our exchange. I'm sure he was only ninety-nine-percent convinced it was nothing more than playful banter.

"His name is Akil Badash," I said. "He's Tunisian."

"Anything else you can tell me? Last known address? Is he still in France?"

"He lived in La Cite on and off with the girlfriend until he disappeared. She said she hasn't seen him in three months. If he has fled the country, can you still track him through his passport?"

"Theoretically, yes. It depends where he exited the country. If he traveled over land, the immigration officers don't scan every passport or have the capability to. If he flew out of Charles de Gaul, yeah, there'll be a record, and I can request passenger manifests from the airlines on that day."

"So we'll know where he went."

"We'll know the destination of the plane. Once he debarks, he can travel over land into another country."

"I'll be waiting for good news."

"Okay, but you know how this works. I'll dig around, but I can't promise I'll find anything on this guy or get a hit on his passport, but—"

"I know, I know. The fact that you're looking into it commits me to owing you another favor."

"Yup."

"You should know that this arrangement works the other way too."

"What do you mean?"

"I mean, if you ask me to steal something, and I try but fail, that still counts as a favor."

"You're too good to fail."

Chapter 15

My cell phone woke me a little after three in the morning. It was Kostas.

"I've got information for you."

"That was fast."

"I got a hit on Akil's passport. He left the country three months ago on an Emirates flight to Vietnam."

"Hmmm."

"Did the girlfriend mention anything about that?"

"No, but I can pay her another visit and ask if he ever spoke of traveling there. What city did he go to?"

"Ho Chi Minh City."

"As in Saigon?"

"That's right. Remember, this only confirms that he was on the flight. Once there, he could have made his way to one of the surrounding countries. He could be anywhere. Laos, Cambodia, China, Thailand—the immigration officials at those border posts usually don't bother to log every single passport they touch. I mean, this guy could be in Pakistan by now."

"Great," I said with annoyance.

"Don't listen to me. Until you chase the lead down,

there's hope. Akil might have mentioned Vietnam to his ex. If that's the case, he's most likely still there." Kostas must have sensed the spinning wheels in my head. "What are you thinking?" he asked.

"Well, I find it odd that a North African immigrant living in France would suddenly pack up and fly halfway around the world to Vietnam."

"He doesn't strike you as a travelholic?"

"Far from it. Somehow I get the feeling that he's on the run or at least not wanting to be found."

"And you're absolutely sure the ex-girlfriend has no idea where he is?"

"When I speak with her again, I'll press harder."

"I thought you would have done that the first time around."

"Something about Akil still had her on edge. I thought keeping the visit gracious would be more productive."

"Probably an abusive a-hole. It's safe to say she doesn't want to give him a chance to come back."

"Maybe, but I think it's something more than that."

"Speaking of—"

"That's your segue? Speaking of? You really do need to work on those transitions."

"Yeah, well good or bad, you're not going to like what I have to say."

"What?"

"I'm guessing since you haven't mentioned it, you

haven't heard about Delacroix."

"Stop running your mouth and get to the point."

"He's dead."

"How? When?"

"Earlier in the evening. Jumped from his balcony, only he had a rope tied around his neck when he did. When the rope snapped tight, it severed his head. His body fell to the pavement below and left his head swinging in the breeze. It's all over the local news. Spectacular way to die if that's what he was shooting for."

"That doesn't sound like him."

"The spectacular part?"

"No, the killing-himself part. He always struck me as a coward. People like that don't have the will to take their life."

"The police are ruling it a suicide. He left a note saying he was sorry—Sei, I'm sorry for you. I know he was a connection to your daughter, and you thought he could still be helpful in finding her."

"I did." Delacroix was helpful only when I had new information that I might jog his memory. I had planned on paying him another visit and discussing Akil with him. It was always one step forward and two steps back.

Chapter 16

The following morning, I took a taxi back to La Cite. Same procedure as the day before: the taxi dropped me off at the entrance to the complex, and I walked in on foot. I hoped my second visit with Akil's ex wouldn't end with a door slamming in my face.

I double-stepped it up the stairs to the seventh floor. The elevator worked but I hadn't had a decent workout in a week and my body needed the exercise. I could feel a stronger beat inside my chest, and my breaths were more forceful than usual. It felt great to feel that type of adrenaline coursing through my veins as opposed to the fight-for-my-life type.

I was dressed in the same outfit as the day before and kept my sheathed knife tucked into my waistband. I knocked on the door to apartment 718. There was movement in the peephole, and I expected to hear the sound of two deadbolts unlatching. Instead, I heard nothing. After waiting a few seconds and concluding that I was being ignored, I knocked again.

"I found him," I said through the door.

A few seconds later, the deadbolts were unlocked, and

Akil's ex-girlfriend shoved her face into the crack. "What do you want from me? Should I be happy?"

"No, but I do need your help again."

"Why? You just told me you found him."

"Did Akil ever talk about Southeast Asia?"

She crinkled her brow. "Is that where he is?"

"It's a strong possibility. Do you remember him mentioning it?"

She thought for a second. "He talked about Cambodia."

"Did he ever mention Vietnam?"

"Maybe. I'm not sure. I always get those countries mixed up. Did he go to Vietnam?"

"Yes. I'm trying to find out if he remained there or traveled to another country. Maybe he flew to Vietnam and then traveled to Cambodia."

She shrugged.

I thought more about what might have her so frightened that she continued to hold back. And then an inkling bubbled up in my head. "Did Akil hurt your daughters?"

"Why do you say that?"

"Look, I'm here to help you. Akil is a bad man. That's why I need to find him."

She chewed on her bottom lip and shook her head slowly. She let out a breath and then opened the door wide enough so she could slip out. She shut it behind her and then proceeded to tell me that Akil had molested her oldest daughter.

"She was only twelve." Her eyes welled up, and she used the back of her hands to wipe them dry. She was unable to look me in the face as she elaborated on what Akil had done.

"Did you report him to the police?"

"Yes, but they didn't do anything," she said, staring at the stained floor in the hall. "I kicked him out and changed the locks."

"I think I know why he talked about Cambodia then. It's a hotbed for men who like sex with underage girls, especially children."

"But you said he went to Vietnam."

"It happens there too, but not to the degree that it does in Cambodia. Maybe he flew to Vietnam and then traveled to Cambodia. He could be in either country, but knowing this about him, that he's a sicko, it'll help me track him down."

She looked up at me. For the first time since we met, I saw hope in her eyes instead of despair.

"Promise if you find him, you make him pay," she said.

I nodded, and she then threw her arms around me. I hugged her back. Which was highly unusual for me, but I felt a connection to this woman. Someone had hurt the person that meant the most to her in the world, her daughter. Someone had stolen the one thing that meant the most to me, my daughter. Even after I felt her grip loosen, I hugged her a little longer, and then I released her.

"Yesmine Mami," she said softly. "That's my name."

"My name is Sei."

I thanked her for her time and watched her close the door before turning and heading for the stairs. When I exited the building, I removed my cell phone to start the process of getting in touch with Kostas. I wanted to see what he thought of the new information I had gained.

After I hung up, I thought about the promise I made to Yesmine. It was one I would keep. Akil would pay for what he did to her daughter and for his role in my daughter's kidnapping.

Just as I took another step forward, I heard a woman shriek. I looked up and saw Yesmine falling from her seventh-floor balcony. She landed with a loud thud a few feet away from me. I couldn't believe what I had just witnessed. I looked back at her balcony just in time to see a man's head vanish from my view.

Chapter 17

Nooooo!

I raced back into the building. My brain scrambled to make sense of what had just taken place; it was only a minute ago I stood in the hall hugging Yesmine. Was that really her on the pavement? Of course it was. I didn't need to turn the body over. I recognized the clothing.

I had a strong suspicion that the man I saw on the balcony was the same person who attacked me and Feki. Who else could it be? But why would he kill Yesmine? Wasn't I the target a few nights ago? None of it made sense.

On my way up, I could hear his shoes clomping down against the stairs, and then the sound stopped. I looked up the middle of the stairwell and saw him peeking at me. Our eyes met; he grinned and then reversed course. I continued up the stairs to the floor where I had seen him.

At the end of the hall I spotted an open window. An old sofa blocked the middle of the hallway, but I cleared it easily with a one-handed vault. When I reached the window, I stuck my head out and saw him sliding down a drainpipe anchored to the side of the building.

I threw a leg over the windowsill and climbed out.

With both hands gripping the pipe, I pressed my feet against the wall and then hand over hand, I lowered myself down the pipe. By the time my feet hit the ground, the killer had run to the front of the building and rounded the corner. When I got there, I saw him running across the field toward the abandoned building he had used as a sniper's nest the previous night. A crowd had already gathered around Yesmine's body.

I crossed the field, sprinting as fast as I could. He ran straight into the building, which I couldn't understand, unless he knew something I didn't. I could hear his footsteps in the stairwell. I looked up through the middle and saw flashes of his hand holding the railing.

At the fourteenth floor, the stairwell to the next floor had collapsed, so I ran into the hall, the only direction he could have gone. The far end of the hallway opened into nothing, as the entire wall was missing due to the partial demolition of the building. I watched the last of him leap out of view.

When I reached the opening, there was a narrow space about eight-feet wide that split the building in half. On each side were small, decorative window balconies. He was jumping back and forth between them as he made his way down the building.

I leapt to the window balcony opposite me. My hands gripped the railing and the balls of my feet landed against the wall. I looked at the balcony that was one floor down, opposite me, and pushed off, twisting my body around and landing on it. I repeated the same move floor by floor until I reached the ninth floor.

That was where I saw him enter the building again through an open window. Before he disappeared from my sight, he laughed out loud and shouted with a French accent, "Catch me if you can!"

He was obviously skilled in parkour, but so was I. I entered the building and faced a hall filled with broken concrete columns positioned at various angles. I hand-vaulted over the first one and then ran along the wall to get around a second beam.

Up ahead, two slabs of concrete were leaning against each like the letter A, but there was no opening below the arch, just a tiny triangle at the top. I dove forward, arms straight ahead, head tucked between them, body straight as an arrow and hoping the jagged concrete wouldn't snag my knapsack. I threaded the opening perfectly. As soon as I cleared it, I tucked in and performed a shoulder roll, rising up to my feet.

The man stood twenty-five feet away with his hands resting on his hips. I suspected he had thought I would take longer to crawl through that opening. He laughed again and then yelled something in French that I was unable to comprehend before disappearing around a corner.

I rounded the same corner, and the hall ended a short five feet away. There was an open window. I looked out and

saw him directly below me, dropping from one windowsill
to another. I swung my body out, hanging on to the
windowsill by my fingers. *Here we go.* I released my grip
and caught myself on the windowsill directly below. He was
moving fast. Faster than I felt I could. Mistime a move and
the drop to the pavement below would be my last.

　When he reached the fifth floor, instead of dropping to
the fourth-floor window, he jumped backward into a
somersault and landed on a flat slab of concrete. The top
floors of the adjacent building had completely collapsed, the
building folding upon itself like an accordion.

　I performed the same reverse somersault maneuver
when I reached the fifth floor windowsill. I crossed the wide
expanse of uneven concrete, jumping over large holes and
skirting jagged columns.

　He started taking bigger risks with his jumps, landing
on one foot, pushing off and landing on the other foot. I
stuck with two-footed landings and that allowed him to pull
further away from me. It was reckless, even if he were
familiar with the terrain. He could wrongly estimate the
distance between steps and come up short.

　And he did.

　He jumped diagonally over a large opening in the
concrete and fell short. His chest hit the edge, and both arms
slapped down hard, but he had nothing to grab hold of. The
momentum from the jump carried his legs up and under the
ledge, and he slipped right off.

When I reached the opening, he had just started to leap across, I looked down and saw him lying on his back. The fall wasn't that high, maybe six feet at the most. Enough to tweak an ankle if he landed wrong but not necessarily kill him. He was still alive as his chest was heaving up and down, but he wasn't moving. I climbed down, and as I got closer to him, I realized why.

He had impaled himself on a piece of rebar. It had punctured his body on the right side of the torso, just below the ribcage in the fleshy area. About three inches of rusted steel stuck out of his body. Even though he still had that silly grin on his face, it wasn't enough to mask the obvious pain he was experiencing.

I knelt next to him. "Who sent you after me?"

He laughed forcefully and then resumed his labored breathing. "No one."

I placed my knee on his torso and leaned forward, forcing the steel to penetrate him more.

His eyes slammed shut, and cry of pain escaped his mouth. His staccato breathing increased. "Stop! Stop!"

"Answer my question."

He lay there, turning his head sided to side as he whimpered.

"I'm not a patient woman." I continued to apply more pressure.

"Okay, stop. Give me a moment."

I eased off.

His breathing remained forceful and fast. "I'm not after you."

I started to move forward again.

"Wait! It's the truth. Midou Feki was my target."

"Why was a contract placed on him?"

"They all have contracts."

"I don't understand. Who are they?"

"The people who worked at the clinic. The day you gave birth. A bounty has been placed on everyone involved."

And then the realization hit me. Delacroix didn't commit suicide; he was murdered. So was Feki.

"Did the Wolf order these hits?"

He nodded.

By eliminating everyone involved, the Wolf was adding another layer of insurance to prevent me from finding him or my daughter. He had decided to tie up all loose ends.

"Are you the only assassin working for him?"

"I don't know. I was given the contract for Feki. He was worth twenty thousand euros."

"Why did you kill Yesmine? She had nothing to do with this."

"Eh, it's a bonus. If we find someone else trying to help you, it's worth an extra five thousand euros. She looked like she was helping you."

"You saw her talking to me, and you assumed she was

helping?"

"Please don't insult me. You and I both know the only people you talk to are the ones who can help." He coughed, and a splatter of blood appeared on his lips.

"Is my name on that list?"

"No."

"Why did you target me?"

"I got caught up in the moment. No hard feelings, eh?"

"I see." I looked at the piece of metal sticking out of him. "It must hurt."

He looked at his wound and shrugged. "I've had worse."

"It's not life threatening, yet." I looked around. I guessed from the chunks of stairs mixed in with slabs of broken concrete, the space we were in used to be a stairwell. "You could climb out of here. It wouldn't be difficult, even with your injury."

"I just need to be lifted off of this...ah, spear."

"Now there's the conundrum—freeing yourself from the spear, as you call it."

He laughed nervously.

"Wait, you aren't thinking I could help you, are you? Why, I think you are." A large smile appeared on my face. I reached up and pinched his cheek. "Aww, you're too funny."

I stood and started climbing.

"Wait, I'll split the bounty with you—sixty/forty. What

do you say?"

"You're generous," I said, looking down at him before pulling myself out of the hole. I picked up a chunk of concrete about the size of a large bowling ball and walked back to the opening.

"What are you doing? Wait!"

I lifted it above my head.

"I'll give you everything. Just don't—"

Chapter 18

Somewhere in the Caucasus Mountains of Azerbaijan

Vasili Ivanovich sat slightly slouched, but his broad shoulders still ran the width of the throne-like chair made of solid cherry. Brass rivets adhered brown leather to the top of the cherry arms, the back, and the seat. On the outer sides of each armrest were detailed carvings of a forest like the dense woods surrounding the compound. An ornate wooden header topped off the back of the chair with similar carvings but added to the forest scene was a shirtless man clenching onto the back of a large bear and driving a knife into the animal.

Opposite Ivanovich, in a similar chair, sat the Black Wolf. He too was a large man with his muscular frame hovering steady at the two-hundred-pound mark. The wooden header on his seat depicted a muscular wolf howling on a mountaintop. Ivanovich had personally handcrafted the furniture. It had taken him two months to get the carvings just right.

The chairs were positioned in front of a roaring fireplace with a large brick mantle. The lights were off in the room, but the flames cast plenty of light. The fire, however, created harsh shadows on each man's face, enhancing every angle and crevice. In anticipation of winter, both men had allowed their beards to flourish. The Wolf pulled methodically on the black growth under his chin. On the floor in front of them was the skin of a large brown bear, including the head and four paws. Ivanovich had conquered the beast earlier in the year.

This was Wolf's personal sitting room. The only other person he'd ever invited inside the room was Ivanovich—his closest confidant and second in command. The two would often sit quietly, drinking vodka and eating pickles as they stared into the dancing fire and listened to the crackling wood. Ivanovich always waited for his boss to initiate conversation.

The Wolf grabbed the vodka bottle and refilled both glasses. "*Afiyet oslun!*" They both downed the liquor in one gulp, and then the Wolf slapped his hands on his thighs. "Talk to me, Vasili."

"Remy Delacroix has been taken care of."

"The doctor?"

"Yes, as was Midou Feki."

"Who is that?"

"He worked as a security guard at the clinic."

The Wolf nodded.

"The assassin who fulfilled the contract said Sei was talking with Feki when he executed him."

The Wolf crinkled his brow, causing the skin to pucker around the large scar that ran across his forehead. "Sniper rifle?"

Ivanovich nodded. "About a hundred and fifty yards out. He told me she gave chase, but he escaped without any problems. He assured me his cover is still secure. He also texted me a picture of a woman a day later—a bonus contract he intended to go after. He said Sei spoke with her after meeting with Feki."

"Who is she?"

Vasili shrugged. "He believes she's the girlfriend of Akil Badash, a member of the team at the clinic. His contract is still open."

"What does Akil know about us?"

"That I'm unsure of. The team leader hired him. He knew the rules about discussing our involvement, but conversations have a way of slipping out. Of course, you know my feeling on this entire matter."

"I do, Vasili."

"Why waste effort and money on these other people? Sei is the threat. We should get rid of her and be done with it."

"You think she is that easy of a target?"

Ivanovich scratched the side of his hooked nose before resting his squared jaw in his palm. "She is one person. We are many."

"Do not underestimate her."

"What is it about her? If it were anybody else, we would have wiped them off this planet."

"I don't want her dead, yet."

Vasili didn't understand why his boss had decided to spare her life, but he left the subject of Sei alone.

"And the others?" the Wolf asked.

"Those contracts are still open."

The Wolf rested his chin on his thumb while he slowly moved a finger back and forth across his lips.

"I want you to put a man on Sei."

"Finally!" Vasili slapped a hand on the armrest. "We'll put our best on her. She'll be no match for—"

"No, she is not to be touched. We stick to the plan. She has information. She might know where a target is located. Let her hinder her own efforts by leading us to this person."

"All right." Ivanovich stood up.

"Vasili, she is not to be touched. Is this clear?"

Ivanovich nodded and headed toward the door. As he opened it, a gray-haired *babushka* appeared. She wore a light blue skirt that fell below her knees and a white blouse. A slightly tattered apron was tied around her waist. She had a meek posture and held her hands clasped in front of her. "I'm sorry to disturb you, but the little one wanted to say goodnight before bed."

Vasili looked back at the Wolf for an answer.

"Bring her in," he said.

A second later, a little girl appeared in the doorway.

She had a large toothy grin and straight black hair that hung to her shoulders. She wore panda-themed pajamas and carried a doll in one hand.

The Wolf smiled at the little girl and patted his lap. "Come here, Mui." When he'd learned that Sei intended to give her that name, he'd kept it.

She ran toward him with open arms. "Papa!"

Chapter 19

Phnom Penh, Cambodia, specifically the district of Svay Pak, was infamously known as the epicenter for child prostitution. The small fishing village on the outskirts of Phnom Penh had garnered a lot of media attention due to a documentary on mothers who sold their daughters into the sex trade, not once, but multiple times. When Yesmine confirmed that Akil had mentioned Cambodia, my inclination was that he had decided to indulge further in his sick behavior. If that was the case, why fly to Vietnam and not Cambodia?

I decided to read up on Svay Pak; perhaps there was a reason that would explain Akil traveling to Vietnam. Turned out, there was a possible, maybe even likely, reason. Most of the people who lived in Svay Pak were ethnic Vietnamese, and many of the young girls working in Svay Pak brothels were from Vietnam. That might explain why Akil had flown to Vietnam. Had Akil gotten himself involved in trafficking? The more I read about Svay Pak, the more I began to despise that man. I also couldn't help but wonder if he had any further contact with my daughter after her birth. *Did he touch her?* There wasn't any doubt in my mind that I would keep the promise I made to Yesmine.

If trafficking was the reason for Akil's travels to Vietnam, I needed more information and I knew exactly where I might find it—the Deep Web—an area of the Internet where ninety-five percent of people who surf never go. It was a hotbed for illegal activity because that was where anonymity thrived. It was also where people in my line of work could find contracts or offer our services. I knew the Deep Web all too well.

I had already been using my TOR browser on my smartphone to surf the web anonymously, so I navigated to the area where numerous boards and chat rooms focused on child prostitution flourished. Even with anonymity, I knew it would be difficult convincing people to talk to me.

Newbies in any forum having to do with illegal activity had to prove themselves. In my profession, word of mouth and recommendations played a vital role. It was fairly easy to sniff out law enforcement pretending to be one of us. I figured this community had also honed its skills in deciphering who was a true participant.

My cover was a man interested in taking his first trip to Southeast Asia, and my question was whether I should visit Vietnam instead of Cambodia because of the recent news stories. My initial posts were either ignored or generic answers, telling me not to worry and go to Phnom Penh. No one wanted to engage any further. Eventually a member of the MLC forum, an acronym for men who love children, provided me with useful information.

I had relayed to him my concerns about visiting Svay Pak, or Phnom Penh in general, because of the recent documentary and that I had heard that Ho Chi Minh City could satisfy my needs.

YungLover: What are you looking for?
Me: Girls. Ages 10-15.

I figured since Akil had molested Yesmine's older daughter and not the younger one, he was interested in that age range.

YungLover: Older isn't a problem in Ho Chi Minh. There's a bar in Phu Nhuan District called Bar 92. Talk to a man named Trang. He can help.

I asked a few more questions but got no replies. It didn't matter. What I had learned so far was compelling enough to book a flight to Vietnam: Svay Pak was a known hotbed for brothels specializing in underage girls. There was a bar in Ho Chi Minh City where young girls could be had. Akil had flown to Vietnam.

The picture forming in my head told me he flew to Ho Chi Minh City to further indulge in his sick fetish and possibly get involved in the human trafficking trade. I was willing to wager it all that he hadn't left.

Chapter 20

A few days later I sat on a Vietnam Airlines flight heading to Ho Chi Minh City. After sixteen hours, my flight touched down at Tan Son Nhat International Airport at eleven a.m. As usual, I traveled light, just a knapsack containing a few changes of clothes and personal amenities. Whatever else I needed I could buy on site. With the crackdown on airport security, traveling with a small pistol or even a garrote wire in checked luggage posed too much of a risk. A knife could easily be purchased at my destination, and I could make do with just that.

I cleared immigration without any problems; I used a Belgian passport I had made over a year ago. My alias was Sophie Bouchon. Ironically, no had ever questioned why an Asian looking woman had a French surname, but I didn't expect to have any problems in Vietnam. The French had occupied the country for years, and aspects of the culture still thrived, particularly in Hanoi.

As I exited the terminal, the wet heat clung to me instantly. The short wait in the taxi queue had me pulling my hair into a ponytail to keep the nape of my neck cool.

I hopped into a cab and headed to the Phu Nhuan

District, where I had booked a room at a small hotel. The drive there was short, only ten minutes, but "chaotic" was a better description. Motorbikes occupied almost every square inch of paved road; cars were the minority. These fearless, medical-mask-wearing riders zoomed and zigzagged with the bravado only a person raised on a bike could have. At times only a few inches separated my door from a two-wheeler carrying a man, woman and two small children.

By the time I checked into my hotel, and searched for and purchased a suitable knife, it was nearing two in the afternoon. By then I had already located Bar 92 with the help of Google Maps. It was tucked away on a small side street just off of Le Van Sy Street, a main throughway that cut through Phu Nhuan. I estimated it would take ten to twelve minutes to walk there, but I wanted to familiarize myself with the neighborhood first, should I find myself in a position where I was on the run.

Phu Nhuan was the most densely populated district in the city with a little over one hundred eighty thousand people packed into an area no larger than four square kilometers. Geographically, it was also the most central district in relation to all the others. There were twenty-four districts in total. Retail shops or restaurants lined nearly every single road I walked along. Apartments, or alley houses, were found in the maze of alleys that branched off from the roads. I learned from my walk that these alleys could abruptly end, loop back around, and split into smaller walkways, where passage was attainable only by foot. One thing that became clear was that very few of them opened to a road on the other side of the block.

I arrived at Bar 92 a little later in the afternoon. I slowed my pace as I walked on the footpath opposite the bar, pretending to window shop at stores selling shoes and handbags. I didn't think barging in and asking about Akil would serve me advantageously.

I continued my little ruse until I reached the corner of the block where I ducked into a twenty-four-hour convenience store and purchased bottled water. The walk had me wiping my forehead every few feet and fluffing my top to remain cool. When I emerged back outside, I was convinced the bar had no security. By all accounts, it appeared to be another business lining the street. I gulped the water as I made my way back toward it.

Directly across the street was a small coffee shop. During my walk over, I had passed a dozen others; most were small and situated in open spaces with a few chairs and tables placed on the sidewalk. This one in particular had an enclosed storefront and air conditioning blowing inside—a nice welcome and one that would suit my needs. Much like the other coffee shops, it was empty, except for the young girl working behind the counter. That was fine by me. I disliked crowds. My plan was to take the long and usual approach: wait for Akil to show up.

I ordered an iced *Ca phe*, Vietnamese coffee, and then

took a seat near the window. A few minutes later, the girl placed two glasses on my table. One had been filled with half an inch of sweetened condensed milk. Balancing on top was a French drip filter filled with a dark roast of grounded Vietnamese-grown coffee. Ice filled the other glass.

I waited patiently as the hot water worked its way through the filter, dripping into the glass and creating a dark layer that floated on top of the milk. When the last of the liquid dripped from the filter, I removed it and stirred the coffee and the milk together before pouring it into the ice-filled glass.

Sweet with a kick, the caffeine-infused elixir was a nice relief from the sticky weather that still seemed to be clinging to me. The weather in Vietnam during the fall months wasn't as scorching as the summer, but considering I had just come from Paris, where the average day temp hovered in the mid-sixties, my internal thermostat wasn't prepared for the drastic change. I fluffed my top once again to help the wet spots in front dry faster.

Bar 92 looked like a typical dive bar. It had a single entrance and no windows. The signage was small, almost invisible, perhaps for a reason. I imagined most of the square footage inside was made up in length and not width. This was typical of most businesses in the area.

As inconspicuous as the bar was, there was a fair amount of activity for that time of the day. I watched a number of men of various ethnicities walk through the front door—each one alone. I highly doubted they had a cold beer on their minds.

On average, the men stayed for a little over an hour, and they all left as they had arrived: alone. Brothel owners almost never let their girls leave the property. And that was exactly what the owner of this bar was. He sold sex. Beer was an afterthought. I suspected the upper floors were also owned by the same establishment, outfitted with small private rooms containing a bed/mattress and a bathroom, either sectioned out by thin walls or even just curtains.

I shifted in my chair while crossing a leg over the other. I had already finished my coffee and had contemplated ordering another when the girl from behind the counter appeared next to my table. I hadn't paid much attention to her since my arrival, but I noted that she looked a little too young to be managing the shop on her own. *It's Wednesday, why aren't you in school?*

"Would you like something else?" she asked with almost no accent.

"No, but thank you. Your English is good."

"Oh, thank you," she said with a smile as she cleared the dishes from my table. She had straight black hair that she kept pulled back in a ponytail, wore no makeup, and hadn't yet worried about grooming her eyebrows. She wore jean shorts, a fashionable T-shirt, and pink and white tennis shoes.

"Did you learn in school?"

"A little," she said as she took the dishes and put them in a sink behind the counter. "There are videos on YouTube that teach for free, and I watch a lot of American TV."

Her determination impressed me. "That explains why you speak so conversationally."

"Conversationally?" She crinkled her brow as she walked back to my table with a cloth in her hand.

"It means you can easily carry a conversation."

"Oh, I'm so happy to hear that. I try and practice every day."

"Keep it up." I watched her wipe my table. "What's your name?"

"My name is Phuong? And you?"

I stuck my hand out. "Sei."

She quickly wiped her hand dry on the oversized apron she wore before grasping mine. "Nice to meet you. Do you have Facebook? We can be friends."

I chuckled. "Sorry, I don't."

"Oh, okay."

She smiled but she probably thought I was weird not to be tuned into social media.

"Do you come to Vietnam for holiday or work?"

"I'm here on business."

"I see you looking at the bar across the street. Are you waiting for someone?"

"Do you know what kind of bar it is?"

She hesitated and then nodded. "Everyone around here

knows what kind of bar it is."

"Really?" I hadn't planned on questioning the girl, but she appeared to be knowledgeable about the bar.

I pulled up a picture of Akil on my cell phone. "Have you seen this man before?" From the look on her face, I already knew her answer. "It's okay. You're not in trouble."

She hesitated again, her eyes shifting to the bar before settling on me.

"I'm not here to hurt you. Sit down." I pulled the chair out next to me. "I need to find this man. He's very bad."

"Yes, he his." There wasn't any hesitation this time. She scooted to the edge of the seat and leaned forward. "I don't like him."

"Did he hurt you?"

She shook her head. "He came into my shop when I was alone. He wanted me to have a drink with him. I kept telling him no, I was too young, but he wouldn't leave. I was very scared."

"What happened?"

"Some other customers came into the shop and he left. I've seen him across the street. He goes into that bar; that's why I was scared of him."

"Do the police know what goes on inside there?"

"Yes, but they don't do anything about it. A very bad man owns the bar, and everybody stays away from him. Sei, don't go inside there. It's not safe for women."

"I appreciate your concern, but he doesn't frighten me.

I'm not afraid of anybody."

Chapter 21

Trang Ngõ sat behind a cluttered desk in a tiny office located on the second floor of Bar 92. He inherited the building and the bar during a dispute that didn't end well for the previous owner. Ever since then, Trang worked hard to breathe new life into the business. He did so by adding new menu items—girls between the ages of ten and fifteen. He wouldn't deal with product younger than that age range, even though his customers continually asked for it.

Girls under ten brought on a slew of problems: law enforcement in Ho Chi Minh City was less tolerant; they were prone to sickness and required more care; and lastly, he just never understood the attraction. His girls were required to have pubic hair.

Trang was busy stabbing his fat forefinger against the number pad of a large plastic calculator while flipping through a stack of receipts on the desk. A newly lit cigarette dangled from his mouth, and wisps of smoke kept his left eye squinted. A thin mustache sat above his lip, and under his chin, protruding from a mole, was single black hair about three inches in length. He never had cut it, considering it to be an omen for good luck.

Trang was not tall in stature and was not in the greatest physical shape. He had a potbelly, chained-smoked, and had terrible hair. Those physical attributes also made Trang look like anything but a threatening man. No, his menacing reputation was a result of his quick-fuse temper, coupled with his lack of remorse. He solved problems with a machete. When that didn't work, he used two. Trang stomped twice on the floor with heel of his left shoe.

On the first floor, standing behind the bar countertop was Trang's closest confidant, Vu Danh. He was also responsible for ensuring that the machetes were always razor sharp. He had his nose buried in a newspaper spread out in front of him and barely glanced up at the ceiling before shaking his head.

Sitting at a table across from the bar were two Vietnamese men, early fifties. They were drinking Bia Saigon and playing cards. They too glanced up at the ceiling, but unlike Vu, they laughed, for they knew exactly what the stomping meant. Vu ignored the request for his presence and continued to read his newspaper.

Vu couldn't have looked any more the opposite from Trang. He wore thick-framed glasses, had his hair slicked back and kept his face clean-shaven. He was rail thin, always wore a white dress shirt with a black tie, and had a knack for disposing of bodies. His work had earned him a nickname: the Magician.

The two met when they were only teens. Vu was the

odd-looking lanky outsider. Trang was the funny fat boy. It was unlikely that the two would ever become best friends, but a chance crossing made that all possible.

After a long night of drinking with a few friends, Trang had ridden his motorbike home. The roads in the Phu Nhuan District were desolate during the wee hours of the morning. Not a soul, not even a dog could be seen—just rats scurrying along the sidewalks.

As fate determined, he had fallen asleep while riding the motorbike and slammed into the back of a parked car. By all accounts, the impact should have killed him but he survived thanks in part to his drunkenness and the fact he was asleep. Had he tensed up before hitting the car, doctors said, the damage would have been much more severe.

Lying on the side of the road and unable to move, Trang should have bled to death. While the impact was noisy, it didn't wake anyone, not even the homeless drunk sleeping fifteen feet away. But Trang would survive that night, all because Vu was an awkward teen without a girlfriend.

At the time, Vu happened to be on the rooftop of his building, gazing at the stars while furiously masturbating for the second time into a pair of panties he stole from his neighbor's clothesline. The impact of the crash had grabbed his attention, enough to make him stop and look over the low wall at the edge of the roof.

A man was lying on the road with his leg bent at an

abnormal angle. Vu carried on with his masturbation, as he was nearly at that point, but when he finished, he went downstairs to check on the man. From then on, the two had been inseparable.

Once again, two stomps echoed throughout the first floor and dust fell from the ceiling. Vu exhaled loudly and folded his paper. He looked around the bar. It was just him, the two old-timers, and a bar-back sweeping. He motioned for the young man to take his position behind the bar.

Before Vu could climb the stairs, the front door to the bar opened, letting in a rush of sunlight. Everyone inside squinted. Seconds later the door closed, revealing a white male in his early fifties.

He had most of his hair and a slight beer belly. He wore blue jeans and a white polo shirt.

"Hello," he said as he walked over to the bar.

"Freddy, long time no see," Vu said as he greeted him with a handshake. "The usual?"

"Yeah, and a Bia Saigon. It's hot outside."

Vu snapped his fingers, and the bar-back quickly removed a green bottle from the ice chest behind him. He opened it and set it down on the bar.

Vu picked up a phone on the desk and pressed the number three on the dial pad. "Tell Sheila she's up. Room four."

He turned back to Freddy. "Whenever you're ready," he said, pointing at the ceiling. "I have to see the boss.

Enjoy."

Vu headed toward the stairs and climbed them to the second floor. There were six doors on the second floor. The first one opened into Trang's office. The other five were rooms for their customers. Each room contained a single bed and a small shower. In a storage space at the end of the hall, a lady in her forties sat on a small stool watching TV. Stacked behind her were mountains of clean towels and bed linens. Vu called out to tell her that a customer had been assigned to room four. She nodded, collected a towel, a sheet, and headed to the room.

The girls who worked for Trang lived on the fourth floor. The entire floor had been converted into a large open space. There were ten beds, two bathrooms, one with a shower, and a kitchen. There was also a large flat-screen TV and a couple of couches and chairs.

There was a small apartment on the third floor where the mama-san who watched over the girls lived. The only way to or from the fourth floor was to pass through her apartment. She would make sure Sheila was ready for the customer.

Vu entered Trang's office, closed the door behind him, and took a seat in the chair opposite his desk.

"Business is down this month," Trang grunted.

"Business is down everywhere. It's slow season," Vu responded. "But a customer just came now—Freddy."

"There is no slow season with fucking. I think we need

new product."

"These girls haven't served out their six-month stay. They still have value and can make us money. If we refresh our inventory now, we will lose more money."

Trang leaned back in his swivel chair, folded his hands on top of his belly, and took a pull on his cigarette. "The customers are tired of fucking them. Even Freddy is tired. When was the last time he was here?"

Vu thought for a moment. "Maybe two, three weeks ago."

"You see? He used to come here two times a week, sometimes three. We need fresh pussy. Where is Akil? I haven't seen him in a week."

"I don't know. He hasn't returned any of my phone calls. Hiring this foreigner was a bad decision. He doesn't work hard. And he smells."

Trang laughed. "You should give him deodorant."

"That won't help. You know his kind. They only shower a few times a week."

"Yes, but he is good at getting girls I like. Find him. I want him to do another run right away."

Vu nodded and stood up.

"And I want a virgin, Vu. Make sure he brings me one. I want to start a bidding war."

Chapter 22

It was nearing nine at night. I was halfway through my *Banh mi dac biet*, which was essentially a choice of two meats packed inside a French baguette. I chose crispy roast pork and pork belly. It also came stuffed with generous slathering of liver pâté and the usual toppings: pickled carrots and radish, sliced cucumber, and fresh cilantro. Phuong offered to buy me one from a vendor outside, as she was purchasing one for herself. The shop only had muffins and pastries available. I thanked her and gave her enough money to pay for both sandwiches.

It was perfectly delicious. The baguette had the right amount of flake to its crust, while the inside remained soft and chewy. The last meal I'd eaten was the microwave-heated box served to me on my flight. I had no problem shoving an overly stuffed six-incher into my mouth. Phuong called it quits after eating half of her sandwich.

"I think I'll save the rest for later," she said as she patted her flat stomach.

"Not me," I said through a mouthful.

Throughout my time in the shop, very few people came inside. Some stayed, maybe thirty minutes at the most; the rest opted to take their iced coffee with them. For most of the evening, it was only two of us. "Is business always this slow?"

"No." Phuong said. "Usually we have customers all day. I don't know why today there is not too many."

"Phuong, if you don't mind me asking, why aren't you in school?"

"Oh, we have a break now. Usually I only work a few hours at night and on the weekends, but now I work all day."

"And where are your parents?"

"My father has another shop selling fabric. My mother died two years ago."

"I'm sorry to hear that."

"It's okay."

"Is it just you and your father, or do you have brothers and sisters?"

"I have an older sister; she is studying at the university. When she has free time, she tries to help out with the shop too. But now she has exams, so she can't be here."

"With your father busy with the other store, who takes over here when you and your sister are busy with school?"

"Oh, sometimes my aunt can help out. If she is busy, there is another girl we hire to work here, but my father doesn't like to do that. He says it's expensive."

This was a quintessential family-run business: long hours to eke out meager profits. I felt sorry for Phuong and wondered how much free time she actually had for herself.

"Do you have a boyfriend, Phuong?"

She giggled and looked away. "I'm too young to have one."

She probably was. "Well, there must be a boy you like? You haven't stopped tapping away on your phone since I arrived. Don't tell me those are just your girlfriends you're talking to."

Her face grew red. "Yes, mostly it's my friends, but there is this one boy I talk with. His name is Dao."

"And is Dao handsome?"

She clasped a hand over her mouth and giggled more. "Why do you ask? Do you have a boyfriend?" Her eyes were wide with curiosity.

"No, I don't," I said, laughing. It had been a long time since I laughed like that but something about Phuong made me comfortable enough to lower my guard. She saw a rare part of me that almost no one ever saw. I wondered if it was because I longed to have similar chats about boys with Mui when she was older.

"With that bar across the street, it doesn't seem like it's safe for you to work alone. How old are you? Fourteen? Fifteen?"

"I'm thirteen," she said with a smile and a dose of sass before crinkling her brow. "But I don't like working by myself. I'm always asking my friends to come and visit me."

"Does it scare you?"

"Sometimes, but we have cameras now." She pointed to the two inside the shop and the one outside. "Plus you are here tonight, so I feel okay." She smiled and then looked at her watch. "We will be closing in a half hour."

I popped the last bite of my sandwich into my mouth and brushed my hands before looking back across the street. As I chewed, a man walking toward the bar caught my eye. I watched him carefully, willing him to look my way. *Come on. Turn your head.* And then he did, and I recognized Akil Badash instantly.

"Phuong, I think I see him." I said, motioning with my head.

She looked across the street. "Yes, that's him," she blurted without hesitation.

While his skin color looked noticeably darker, his build matched the one in the photo. He was thin and not very tall, perhaps five feet seven inches. He wore jeans and a simple black T-shirt with a fanny pack strapped around his waist.

He didn't appear to be concerned about anyone looking for him. I figured he was unaware of the contract on his head. Most marks never knew. One minute they were living their lives; the next minute, their skull was shattered by a thirty-caliber bullet. On occasion, a client would demand that the target know they are about to die. Some assassins thrive on this, seeing the fear in the person's eyes before they end his life. I was not one of those types, but I would do it if the job required it.

I had no belongings to grab since I had left my knapsack in my hotel room. The knife I had purchased earlier, a six-inch, fixed-blade hunting knife, was tucked under my shirt into the rear of my jeans, out of sight from prying eyes.

I stood. "Phuong, it's been nice talking with you."

"Oh, I think I'll leave too. Would you mind waiting?"

I nodded.

She locked the back door and then switched off all the lights. After we exited the shop, she pulled down a metal gate and secured it to the pavement with a padded lock.

"Are you going to the bar?" she asked as she put on her helmet and slipped on a pair of gloves.

"No, I'll wait for him to come out."

Phuong straddled the seat on her motorbike and revved the engine. "Be careful, Sei," she said before driving off.

Chapter 23

I waited under the shadows of the coffee shop's awning for Akil to exit the bar. My plan was pretty straightforward—intercept and question, preferably at his apartment. There was still a fair amount of foot traffic on either side of the street, and while the number of motorbikes on the road had diminished, they hadn't disappeared.

It didn't take very long for Akil to show his face again, maybe thirty minutes or so, and he wasn't alone. A young girl exited the bar with him. She couldn't have been older than twelve or thirteen. *Bastard!*

Either Akil had special privileges or he was working for the bar because I saw no other man leave with a girl. Whatever the reason, I wasn't about to let him have his way with her. I waited until he was about thirty feet from the bar before crossing over to his side of the street.

Akil looked to be in his mid-thirties, theoretically old enough to be the girl's father. She walked about two steps behind him with her head down, and he never bothered to look back to see if she was following. Was it trust or fear that kept her from running? Surely she wasn't a willing participant.

The two continued walking along Le Van Sy Street for another hundred yards or so until they reached a women's clothing store that had just closed. There they turned right into a small alley.

When I reached the store, I peeked around the building and saw their outlines up ahead. Akil had taken hold of the girl's hand, but it didn't look like they were talking. I moved ahead. A motorbike zoomed by, but aside from that, the small lane was empty. On either side of the alley were typical Vietnamese homes: narrow, three-story buildings. I heard families talking, television sets playing loudly, children yelling, and the soulful notes of someone belting out a song on a karaoke machine.

I removed my knife from the sheath and held it close to my thigh, anticipating the right moment as Akil led me deeper into the residential area. He rounded another corner and when I reached it, it was much darker. It seemed like the perfect spot to ambush him and set the girl free.

But before I could make my move, someone else did.

Four men appeared from the shadows, and Akil reacted by shoving the girl into the path of the man closest to him. The collision helped Akil to avoid taking a pipe to the face and gave the girl an opportunity to run off.

I moved in quickly, striking the back of the head of the man nearest me with the butt of my knife, causing him to fall to the ground unconscious, his head making a loud thunk as it hit the pavement hard. *One down.* My surprise attack caused enough confusion for the other three men to stop their advances on Akil and focus on me.

The man nearest me stepped forward and swung a wild fist at my face. I jerked my head back, and he connected with air. I wasn't planning on using deadly force, but given it was three against one, I changed my mind. I ducked to avoid his next swing and countered with a swipe of my blade cross his stomach. It cut deep enough for him to back off, clenching his stomach and grimacing in pain.

I wasted no time moving toward the man who wielded the metal pipe. He swung it down at me in a chopping motion. I sidestepped the pipe and delivered an open palm strike to his face, backing him up before following with a straight kick to the left side of his torso.

He doubled over, and I immediately struck the side of his head with my knee. His legs buckled for a second, but he kept himself upright as he wobbled from side to side. I crouched and delivered a swooping leg kick, taking his feet out from under him. He fell to his side, and I stuck the knife into his thigh. His femur stopped the blade.

I turned to face the third man. He held a knife out in front of him and randomly jabbed at me. These were novice fighters. There really was no need to kill; maiming would neutralize the situation. I dropped my defensive stance and smiled at him. "Give me your best shot."

He accepted the challenge and lunged, knife first. I grabbed his hand at the wrist, pushed down, stepped off to the side and slammed the back of my fist straight into his face—not once, not twice, but thrice. The second punch produced blood; the third broke his nose.

He dropped his knife and used his other forearm to shield his face from further strikes. I kicked him in the groin instead and sent him to his knees. I then grabbed the back of his head and drove a knee into his face, snapping his head back and knocking him unconscious.

Two of the men were sleeping on the pavement; the other two were moaning and coddling their wounds. I yanked my knife out of the whimpering man's thigh, but when I turned to look for Akil, he had disappeared.

Chapter 24

I continued down the alley, rounding another corner, sure that Akil hadn't run in the direction we had come from. After ten feet or so, movement in the shadows behind two large trash containers caught my eye. *Akil!*

"Come out from there now!"

He didn't move.

"Surely you don't think I can't see you."

In the distance, I could hear men shouting. "Your friends have reinforcements. The way I see it, you can stay here and deal with this yourself or come with me. I'm not interested in hurting you. I just need information from you."

"Who are you?" Akil asked.

"I'm the person who saved your life."

The shouting got louder. "We're running out of time here."

He came out from behind the trash bin. "I live down this road."

"No, they probably know where you live. Is there another way out of here?"

He nodded. "Yes, follow me."

We ran through a narrow passageway between two

buildings, hopped over a low wall and then continued for another fifteen feet or so before popping into another alley.

"Get us back to Le Van Sy Street, and I can take over from there," I said.

"This way," he said.

A couple of left and right turns and then a long straightaway put us back on Le Van Sy. "Where to now?" Akil asked as he nervously looked up and down the street.

I took over navigational duties and got us back to the safety of my hotel in less than ten minutes. The lobby was empty except for the young woman working the reception desk. She gave us a friendly smile as we entered, even though sweat poured down both of our faces.

"How was your evening?" she asked.

"It was fine thank you. I'll be checking out tomorrow."

"Okay. I'll make a note of that. I hope your stay was enjoyable."

"It was," I said as we walked toward the elevator.

Once safely back in my room and with the door locked behind us, I drew my knife and confronted Akil.

"Hey, hey, you said you wouldn't hurt me."

"I won't unless you give me a reason. Now listen carefully, as I don't enjoy repeating myself. Given the situation, I need to establish a few ground rules." I kicked the chair out from under the desk and motioned for Akil to take a seat.

"Wait, who are—"

"First rule. Don't speak when I'm talking. Ignoring this would be a reason for hurting you. Now sit and listen."

He reluctantly took a seat. I sensed he was still unsure of my threats and that he might test me. I had to hope he wasn't that stupid. But stupid people can be stupid like that.

"Those men who attacked you, who were they?"

He shook his head. "I don't know."

"That wasn't a mugging. It was an ambush—premeditated." I wasn't sure how long I had to remain with Akil, so I needed to know why he was attacked and whether I had to be concerned about it.

"I don't know those men. I've never seen them before."

I didn't think he was being entirely truthful with me but I did think it was possible for him not to know them. There was also the bit about the Wolf putting a contract on his head, though that was what I found confusing. Clearly they weren't professionals. Surely he didn't hire them. But I had been wrong before.

"Those men should have killed you tonight, but they didn't because of me. If you feel safe now, realize it's temporary. Those men will continue to come after you."

"What do you want from me?"

"I'm glad you asked. Rule number two. If you don't help me, I won't hesitate to kill you. Am I clear thus far?"

Akil's posture stiffened. He swallowed hard as his eyes shifted from side to side.

"Whatever plan of escape your tiny brain is conjuring

right now won't work. If I can easily dispatch four men with very little effort, believe me, I can do the same with you."

"I don't know you. How can I help you?"

I quickly reminded him about that day in the clinic, how Delacroix faked the death of my baby.

"You were the woman?"

"Yes, and you played a role in that kidnapping."

"I had nothing to do with that. I'm not a nurse or a doctor. I was hired for security."

"Who hired you?"

"Some man, an Asian man. He said nothing about kidnapping a baby. They told me I would be guarding a very important person. That's it. I didn't even know you were there to have a baby."

"Security. That's it?"

"Yes."

"Well, Akil, it seems you're not as useful as I thought you would be." I raised my knife.

"Wait, wait! Don't hurt me. I can help you."

"How?"

"The Wolf. That's who you're after, right?"

Up until that point, I hadn't mentioned the Wolf's name. "You're withholding information from me, Akil. Not a smart thing to do. How do you know the Wolf?"

"You want him, right? Okay, then you must help me."

"You are not in a position to negotiate with me."

"I have information you need. If you want it, you'll

help me."

"If you are lying to me, Akil, it will be the last lie you tell."

"I promise. I have information. Just help me get away from those men. Help me get out of the country."

You poor fool. "I'll let you in on a little secret, only because you have no idea the trouble you're in. The man behind the kidnapping, the Wolf, he's put a contract on your head."

"What?"

"In an effort to keep me from finding him, he's decided to eliminate everyone involved with the birth." I then told Akil what happened to Delacroix, Feki, and his ex-girlfriend, Yesmine.

Akil's mouth fell open, and he stuttered aimlessly before managing a complete sentence. "She's dead? Are you sure?"

"I watched her fall from her balcony. A professional assassin threw her over the railing, in front of her children. That same assassin also shot Midou Feki in the head with a sniper rifle. I had conversations with both of them shortly before they were killed."

He wiped a hand over his face while his left leg bounced in quick succession. "You're talking to me. That means I'm next. Those men who attacked me earlier…they're assassins?"

"They could be. It's possible they tracked you down

because of me."

"You led them to me?" Akil began to fidget in the chair and rub the top of his thighs.

"Calm down. I don't know that. I'm hypothesizing. But if I found you, so could they."

"You have to help me," he said, holding his hands up as if he were about to pray.

"There's a contract on your head. There's nothing I can do about that. However, I can escort you out of the country."

"Yes. Get me to Cambodia—Phnom Penh—and I'll tell you everything I know about the Wolf."

"Fine. We'll take the first flight tomorrow morning."

"No. We can't fly. I don't have my passport."

I let out a dismissive breath. "What did I tell you about being truthful?"

"I'm not lying. I mean, I didn't know. Everything is moving so quickly. It's hard to think. I'm sorry. But we can get there by bus. It's not far."

"You still need a passport to cross the border."

He shook his head. "We can bribe the immigration guards at the border. I've done it before. It's not hard."

Traveling by bus wasn't ideal. I didn't want to spend any more time with this piece of filth than needed. "Once in Phnom Penh, then what?"

"I give you the information."

Chapter 25

Akil and I talked a bit longer about how we would move over land to Phnom Penh. Out of habit, I wanted to assess the situation and try to prevent any unnecessary surprises, but there was always the chance that he would undermine my efforts.

"I promise you. This is the best way to go," Akil said. "We take a bus from Ho Chi Minh. At the border, we give the bus driver some money, and he'll take care of the immigration officials. It's very easy."

"And then we continue on the same bus to Phnom Penh?"

"Yes. That's it. Simple." Akil stretched his arms out, palms up.

The plan sounded too easy, and easy always had a way of masquerading as impossible.

I took a seat at the foot of the bed, away from Akil, and we sat in silence. I thought about what I was about to agree to, and I didn't like it. I shuddered at the thought of spending more time with this man. He had molested Yesmine's daughter and who knew how many others. He had planned to do the same thing to that young girl he was with earlier. The thought of him doing the same thing to my daughter briefly entered my mind again. My stomach turned. I should have let those men kill him. He'll never stop on his own. Death was the only true rehabilitation available for men like him.

While Akil disgusted me, I had to look at the bigger picture. This wasn't about him; this was about finding my daughter. If helping him brought me one step closer to reuniting with her, then I was willing to make my peace with what I was about to do. There was nothing I wouldn't do to get her back.

"I know what you are," I said, turning my head toward him.

"Huh?" Akil shook off his thoughts. "What are you talking about?"

"I know what you did to Yesmine's daughter. I know why you came to Vietnam. I know what you were planning with that little girl tonight."

He waved a dismissive hand at me and I shot off the bed straight at him. My right fist connected with the left side of his face. *Smack!* I followed with a left and then another right. The last punch knocked him off of the chair.

He lunged forward, arms stretched out to tackle me, but instead I introduced my knee to his face. His head snapped back, and his legs buckled. I jumped onto his chest, straddling him. I had my knife drawn and pressed against his neck.

He was still stunned from my counterattack and wasn't fully aware of how close he had come to losing his life. The way he reacted to my earlier comment angered me to no end. How could he be so matter of fact with something so sickening? I leaned in, my face inches from his. I could feel his hot breath. "Don't ever dismiss me when I speak to you. Is that understood?

He nodded, and I pulled back.

"You are a coward who preys on the weak," I said as I stood up.

"And what are you?" Akil still sat on the floor, leaning back on his hands. "You are like those men who are after me. You kill people. You are no better than me."

"No, that's where you're wrong. I kill people who don't deserve to live, people who contribute nothing positive to this world."

I used duct tape I had purchased earlier to secure his hands behind his back. I then did the same with his ankles and left him on the floor while I took a seat on the bed. We stayed like that until sunrise, a little before six. Akil said the first bus from Ho Chi Minh City to Phnom Penh left at eight fifteen a.m.

I took a quick shower, leaving the bathroom door open as well as the shower curtain, so I could keep an eye on him. I toweled off, changed into my clothes, and then cut Akil's hands and ankles free. "Take a shower. You smell."

Sunlight flooded the room as I pulled the drapes open. I

noticed an envelope had been slipped under the door. It was my checkout notice. I already prepaid for the night so there was nothing we needed to do but leave.

After Akil finished showering, he dressed and walked out of the bathroom. "We need to stop by my apartment so I can get a few items."

"No."

"But I have nothing. No clothes. No—"

"I don't care."

"But I—"

"I'll give you the benefit of doubt and assume, because it's early in the morning, that you're not stupid enough to believe you can safely waltz right back into your apartment to pack a bag after what just happened." I glanced at my watch. "We've got an hour before the bus leaves. How long will it take us to get to the bus terminal?"

"Buses heading out of the country leave from Pham Ngu Lao Street. It'll take us twenty minutes by taxi to get there," he said as he walked over to the window and stared outside. We were high enough that we looked over the adjacent building. Rooftops of homes and apartments as far as we could see.

I swung my knapsack over my shoulders and turned to Akil. That was when I noticed a flash from a rooftop in the distance. "Akil!"

I darted forward and tackled him to the floor just as sniper bullet pierced the window and lodged itself in the opposite wall.

"They're shooting at me! I thought you said those men from last night weren't professionals?"

"They didn't appear to be, but that doesn't mean they weren't. There could be more than one assassin trying to collect the bounty on your head. We can't stay here. We have to leave now."

We crawled on our hands and knees and exited the room. The hotel had six floors, and I led Akil to the stairwell. "That sniper was positioned on the roof of a building about seventy or eighty feet away. You should be dead. That's twice I saved your life. You better have information I can act on."

"What do we do?"

"We need to get out of here. It's too dangerous to stay here any longer."

The stairwell led to a crowded lobby. A group of Chinese tourists were milling around the lobby, most likely heading out on an organized tour.

"Miss Bouchon," said the lady behind the reception desk.

"Yes."

"Will you need transport to the airport?"

"That won't be necessary."

"Are you sure? The hotel has a free shuttle bus."

"We not heading to the airport. Thank you."

We joined the group of Chinese tourists and followed

them out of the hotel.

"Bouchon? Is that your real name?" Akil asked.

"That's of no concern to you," I said, dismissing him quickly. Up until that point, the information I had given Akil was limited, and my name wasn't a part of it.

I kept my eyes peeled, but the truth was I had no idea what the person who shot at us looked like or if he had eyes on us. If it were me at the other end of that rifle, I would have moved in after my first shot missed the target. I had to assume he was on foot.

The Chinese tour group headed toward a large tour bus about twenty feet away. There were a couple of taxis parked in front of it. "Follow me," I said.

We stuck with the group right up until we reached the bus and then peeled away and hurried into the nearest taxi. A few seconds later, the taxi drove out of the hotel parking lot, and we were on our way.

I kept my eyes on the vehicles behind us, but it didn't look as if we were being followed. I glanced at Akil. He tapped a nervous finger on the door handle as sweat leaked down the side of his cheek. "I think we're okay for now," I told him. "But if I were you I'd take my hand off that door handle and dismiss any thoughts you might have about running. You need me to get you out of here alive."

Chapter 26

Piece of junk.

Anzor Mdivani threw the M40 sniper rifle down. *Damn sights are off.* The M40 was the only rifle he could get his hands on in Vietnam on such short notice. It was old and noisy and required a thorough cleaning before he could use it. All along, he knew it was a one-shot rifle; not having sound suppression dictated that. He always carried a Beretta M9, a sound suppressor for it, two extra magazines, and a five-inch tactical knife on his body; all had made it onto the plane in checked luggage without any problems, but he had thought the rifle would do the job.

Mdivani slung a leather knapsack holding his equipment, and a few personal items, and clothing over his shoulders and quickly made his way down from the rooftop. As he approached the hotel, he saw no sign of Sei and Akil, but he hadn't expected to. He knew they were on the move, but he needed information to figure out where they might have gone.

Mdivani mustered his best attitude and entered the hotel lobby. He had a flawless complexion, sea green eyes, a chiseled jaw, large dimples, and brown wavy hair that curled behind his ears—a combination that usually resulted in women eagerly wanting to talk to him. It also helped that he wore a fitted plaid button-down that showed off his broad shoulders and gave clear indication of the washboard stomach behind the fabric. Designer jeans and black boots rounded off the ensemble.

His target was the young woman behind the reception desk. She appeared no older than twenty-five, and her eyes screamed boredom. She was dressed in a red *áo dài*, a form-fitting silk tunic that she wore over white slacks. Her hair was pulled back tightly into a bun, showing off her slender face, high cheekbones, and full lips. Her only makeup was pink lipstick.

"Hello," Mdivani said with a smile and a nod. "I'm hoping you can help me."

"Yes, of course." She smiled back. Her teeth were crooked but pearly white.

Mdivani rested an elbow on the desk, closing the distance between them. "I'm a private investigator from France. A father who is desperately searching for his daughter has hired me to find her. I was led to believe she might be staying at your hotel. Would you mind looking at a picture of her?"

"Oh, I'm sorry to hear that."

He removed his cell phone from his pant pocket and showed her a photo. "Her name is Sei, though she could be using a different name."

The young girl narrowed her brow as she leaned in for a closer look. "Yes, I know this woman, but that wasn't the name she used. It was Bouchon." The woman flipped through a ledger on her desk. "Here it is. Sophie Bouchon. I spoke with her a little this morning. She was with another man. They've already checked out of the hotel."

"I see. She didn't happen to mention where she was heading, did she?"

"No, but I don't think they were going to the airport because the hotel has a free shuttle and she wasn't interested. Is there anything else I can help you with?"

"That will be all. Thank you for your time."

Mdivani exited the hotel and thought about his options. He knew Sei had searched out Akil for information. If he had any to give her, she would have it already and left him long ago. But she hadn't. That meant he probably needed to take her somewhere or to someone. Why else would she remain with the scumbag?

Mdivani started tracking Sei while in Paris, shortly after Feki's death. Thanks to his detailed observation, he felt confident he could closely guess what she was thinking at this moment. He knew from watching her that she didn't appear to be a very social person, and she was extremely logical and strategic. While in Paris, she spoke only to those who would help her cause. Outside of that, she ate alone and kept to herself. If Akil was taking her to a specific place or to meet someone in Ho Chi Minh City, she would have made him do it right away but that didn't happen.

They spent the night in the hotel. That was asking a lot for someone like Sei. She could have easily interrogated Akil on the move. Instead, they stayed put. They were buying time. It was likely they needed to travel outside of Ho Chi Minh City, somewhere a taxi wouldn't be feasible.

If they were planning to leave the city, the next question he had was whether it would be to another location within the country or across the border? Travel options at that point were planes, trains, and buses. Planes were faster—Sei would favor this if at all possible. However, buses were discreet and offered numerous options. Train travel was often slower than a bus and their rigid scheduling eliminated flexibility in travel. Mdivani quickly dismissed the train option.

He chewed his bottom lip as he scanned the hotel parking lot. *Did they take a bus or a plane?* He glanced at his watch. Nearly twenty minutes had passed since he fired his rifle. The longer he stayed put, the greater the chance of losing them. As it stood, he still had an opportunity to catch up with them. He was one of the best at what he did: tracking humans.

From what he gathered, Akil couldn't have been in Vietnam very long. The fact that Sei had traveled to Vietnam only confirmed that she herself thought the trail was still fresh. If Akil were new to the city, his network of associates would most likely be contained to Ho Chi Minh

City. And if that were true, Mdivani figured he could then rule out other cities in Vietnam. That left one option in his mind: they were planning to leave the country.

That still left Mdivani with the transport dilemma. Plane travel was efficient, but it wasn't without its problems. There was heightened security, their passports could be easily tracked, and it involved much waiting. Traveling by bus eliminated most of those problems, and she could easily keep a weapon while doing so. Mdivani assumed Sei had weapons.

Mdivani hurried back inside the hotel lobby to talk to the receptionist. "Excuse me. If I needed to travel outside the country on a bus, what terminal would I go to?"

"Only charter buses travel outside of Vietnam. What country do you want to go to? Laos or Cambodia?"

"Are those the only destinations available?"

"No. You can go to Thailand, but it's a very long ride and you must change buses a lot. It's easier to fly."

"Where can I find a charter bus?"

"There are many." She removed a pamphlet from a drawer. "Here is a list of the travel agencies that can book travel to Laos and Cambodia. You buy your ticket from them and wait for the bus there. They're all in the same location."

"Where is that?"

"Pham Ngu Lao Street."

Chapter 27

We were able to make it to Pham Ngu Lao Street fairly quickly, even with traffic. Akil said it didn't matter which travel agency we used, they all sold the same tickets to the same buses. We got lucky: the next bus leaving for Phnom Penh was scheduled to depart in twenty minutes and tickets were still available.

It wasn't until we were on the bus and on our way that I relaxed a little. Up until then, I expected another attack, considering Akil had been targeted twice in one twelve-hour period. It was unusual for a single assassin to strike that way. It looked like Akil had two separate individuals after him.

However, something about the first attack bothered me. It struck me as a mugging by local thugs. It appeared as if no thought had been put into it. It lacked any sort of coordinated effort to kill Akil, unless their intentions were to subdue him and take him somewhere else.

The second attack had all the marks of a professional hit. A sniper camped at a safe distance with a great deal of patience, as he probably waited all night for those drapes to open. Even though he missed the shot, he would coordinate another attack. At least that was what I would have done if I had missed—but I doubt I would have. With that said, he still needed to track us down. I thought about a possible trail we might have left. There wasn't much. It would be no easy feat.

After we passed the outer edges of the city, commercial and residential buildings quickly gave way to a mixture of rice fields and orchards, punctuated with grazing water buffalo. The bus we were on was a double-decker with curtained and tinted windows. It had all the amenities one could ask for a comfortable ride: air conditioning, personal entertainment systems, and beverage and snack service. The outside of the vehicle told a different story. Plastered on both sides of the vehicle was a colorful mural of anime characters I couldn't identify. It screamed party bus. Akil and I sat toward the rear on the lower level. Most of the passengers opted for the scenic upper level. We were practically alone.

"What else can you tell me about that day?" Akil had been staring out the window, lost in a daydream, when I asked the question. I had to shove my elbow into his ribcage to gain his attention.

"Huh?"

"Tell me more about what you saw that day at the clinic."

"There is nothing more to tell. I was told to stand outside the operating room. I didn't see much."

"How many people were involved? Did you know any of them?"

"I don't know, maybe seven or eight."

"Were you the only one hired as security?"

"No, there was one other man, but I didn't know him. I didn't know anybody."

"How many nurses?"

Akil's eyes shot up and to the left. "I think five. They were all women."

All the information he had given me so far corroborated what Delacroix had conveyed to me about his involvement in the birth. They were both telling the truth for the most part.

"And you're sure you didn't know any of these nurses?

He shook his head. "I told you already."

"Did you see them take my baby from the room?"

"Yes. The doctor and a nurse brought the baby out."

"Where did they take her?"

"Into another room."

"What type of room was it? Did they leave the baby inside there?"

"I think it was just another room where they do operations. They were in there for fifteen minutes before the doctor came out and talked to the man in charge."

"What did this man look like? Was he the one who hired you?"

"I don't know, he had a mask covering his face. I

couldn't hear what he was saying but after they talked, he paid me and told me to leave."

"And the other nurses?"

"I think some left and some stayed longer. I can't be sure because I left the building."

"So far everything you've told me is in line with what I already know."

"You see," Akil said, a smile proudly forming across his face, "I'm not lying to you."

"You may not be, but the problem is you've told me nothing I didn't already know."

As quickly as his smile appeared, it deflated. Akil shook his head and let out a breath. He scratched his chin. "I can't win with you."

"As I said before, I need information I can act on. You haven't given me any. You promised me information on the Wolf."

"When we get to Phnom Penh. This is what we agreed."

"I need to know more now. Do you know his whereabouts? Have you worked with him before or met him?"

Akil's eyes shifted away from mine briefly. He licked his cracked lips, leaving a thin layer of moisture before mumbling something I couldn't understand.

"You don't know any of those things do you Akil? Unless you can answer one of those questions, I'm afraid your time is up." I reached for the knife I had tucked in my waistband.

"Wait, wait. Okay. Just listen to me. I know somebody who knows the Wolf."

I shook my head and clenched my jaw. "Not good enough." I drew the blade from its sheath.

Akil's hands went up in a defensive position. "I swear. She can help you. She was the one who brought your baby out of the room. She held her."

At the mention of those last three words, a shiver of hope radiated outward from my chest to my arms, legs, and back. Akil had pressed the right button. Up until then, Delacroix was the closest connection I had to my daughter. When I found out he had been killed, hope of finding her died with him, but knowing there was another person out there, someone who actually held my daughter... It almost brought tears to my eyes. "Where is this nurse?"

"I'm speaking the truth, but I won't say more until I'm safe."

Akil would never be safe so long as the Wolf had an open contract on him. If escorting him to Cambodia made him think otherwise, I could live with that.

"Is she in Phnom Penh?"

Akil didn't say anything.

"Tell me she's at least in Southeast Asia and not back in France."

"She's not in France."

"Your cryptic answers are testing my nerves. Where is she?" I said, digging the tip of my knife into his side.

Akil gasped. "She's...she's in Thailand."

"Thailand? Really? I think you're lying, Akil. I think you've told me everything you know and are trying to buy yourself time."

"I promise it's the truth."

"You told me slivers of the truth and I've run out of patience."

"I swear, once we get to Cambodia I'll give you her name and where she is."

"Is there anything else I need to know?"

He hesitated then swallowed.

"Akil?"

He took a deep breath and licked his lips again. "I know the men who attacked me last night. They're a Cambodian gang from Phnom Penh."

Chapter 28

I slammed my fist into the headrest of the seat in front of me. "Why on earth are we heading to Phnom Penh? You can't be that stupid?"

Oh, but yes, he is, Sei. Yes, he is.

At that moment, the two attacks completely made sense. Someone other than the Wolf wanted Akil dead. To make matters worse, we were heading straight into the gang's home territory. What they lacked in skill could be made up in numbers.

A large part of me wanted to wipe Akil from my life, even my memory. My frustration with the situation continued to bubble. It seemed as if whenever I thought we had a clear path forward, a roadblock appeared. I gritted my teeth and took a deep breath. I couldn't let these obstacles get to me. *Find a solution. There's always one.* Plus, I had promised myself that I would chase down every lead in the search for my daughter. I couldn't walk away not knowing if what he said about the nurse in Thailand was true.

"Tell me everything about this gang. Why are they after you? How many members do they have? How strong are they? The more I know about them, the better I can protect you. Leave anything out and I cannot promise your safety."

Akil nodded. "They're a big gang in Phnom Penh. They call themselves Khmer Kings, and they hired me to transport girls between Cambodia and Vietnam."

"Why do they want you dead?"

Akil shifted in his seat and then looked out the window at the passing countryside. "A girl died, and they blame me."

"Were you responsible for her death?"

"It was an accident."

The details weren't necessary for me to realize he had most likely killed her during a violent sex escapade.

"We were playing," he said with a flippant shrug. He turned to me. "It was unfortunate."

Smack!

I had thrown a punch straight into the side of Akil's face. "One. What you did to that girl was unfortunate. Two. Don't ever speak about what it is you do as if it were normal."

Akil held his face and crinkled his brow. His eyes bore into me with hate. "You cannot treat me this way," he snipped.

"Be mindful of how you speak to me. This isn't a partnership we have here. There's no equality."

He stared at me for a few seconds longer before reclining his seat, turning his body away from me, and resting his head against the window. I regretted helping him, but it was one of the necessary evils I knew I would have to endure in the search for my daughter. But helping him while knowing what kind of person he was brought out my emotions, something that didn't happened often.

With a Cambodian gang and a hired assassin after Akil, I questioned whether escorting him to Phnom Penh was worth it. I thought briefly about checking into a small hotel and applying other techniques to retrieve the information. But up until that point, he had spoken truthfully about that day in a clinic. That was his saving grace.

We kept to ourselves for the remainder of the ride to the Moc Bai border crossing. It was better that way. It kept me calm, and Akil didn't get punched again.

It took us just under two hours to reach the border crossing. I was a bit surprised at how commercially developed the area was. The way Akil spoke about it, I pictured two guard shacks positioned near an imaginary territory border.

A variety of shops, restaurants, and small hotels lined the road leading to the Vietnamese immigration building: an imposing structure with a wide concrete sweeping rooftop reminiscent of imperial Chinese architecture.

"We get off here and wait in that building," Akil said. "The bus driver will meet with the immigration officials. Afterward, he'll return everyone's passport."

"What happens to you?" I asked.

"We will give the driver some money, and he will take care of it. I will be allowed to leave the building with the rest of the group."

After we paid the driver, we waited inside the building for nearly an hour before he returned with everyone's passports. We exited the building into a free zone between Vietnam and Cambodia. The driver instructed everyone to get on board and proceeded to drive us the fifty yards to the Cambodian immigration building.

The contrast between the two buildings was plainly apparent. The architecture for the Cambodian immigration building resembled that of Buddhist *wats*, temples, found throughout Thailand. It had red-tiled, tiered gable roofs complete with ornate bargeboards and a golden *chofa*, a decorative ornament, sitting on top. The lack of an economic zone outside of the gates was another drastic contrast to Vietnam—flat farmland as far as I could see.

Everyone exited the bus but the driver didn't bother to collect our passports this time around.

"Here everybody must talk to the immigration official," Akil whispered to me as we walked toward the building. "Give me one hundred euros, and I will give it to the official at the counter."

We proceeded into the building and stood in line. Thirty minutes later, I had a tourist visa placed inside my passport. I waited by the exit for Akil, who was still at the counter. Almost all of the passengers from our bus had their passports stamped and were filing out of the building back toward the bus. I looked around for the bus driver and spotted him talking to one of the officials. Just as I started to think Akil might be having a problem, he turned around with a smile and walked toward me.

"Everything is okay," he said.

We exited the building and got onto the bus. When the bus driver returned, he walked toward our seats and pointed back at the office. He had a smile on his face, and he rubbed his forefinger and thumb together. Apparently one hundred euros wasn't enough to allow passage.

"Don't worry. They're just greedy."

I handed Akil another hundred euros and sat back down in my seat but the driver pointed to both of us and to the office.

"Why do we both have to go?" I asked.

Akil shrugged. "In case another hundred euros isn't enough?"

"You'll wait here for us?" I asked the bus driver while pointing at Akil and me and then at our seats.

He smiled and nodded eagerly. "Yes, bus wait. Hurry."

We exited the bus, and no sooner had we taken a few steps than I heard the familiar hissing of the bus's air brakes. I looked back, and the bus had begun to drive away. Akil pounded on the glass door, but the driver ignored him and continued driving, leaving us stranded at the border.

Chapter 29

"What just happened?" I asked, turning to Akil. "Didn't he say he would wait?"

"I think leaving us here was the plan." Akil spun on his heels as he looked around us.

"I saw the bus driver talking to an official earlier who could have something to do with it."

"Anything is possible. Let's get out of the open."

We quickly walked away from the immigration building. "We need another way across the border," he said, leading the way. "Maybe one of the guards operating the gate can be bribed. That one, smoking a cigarette."

A lone guard stood about twenty feet away from the small office that manned the actual gate. He wore a neatly pressed tan uniform and had an AK-47 slung over his shoulder. He looked young, possibly new to the job. In my experience, those individuals weren't always susceptible to bribes, as they seemed to be intent on following the rules, unlike their older counterparts who were over it, but there was always the anomaly.

Three other guards were mingling inside the office, and two more stood next to the gate. All five were engulfed in lively conversation with one another and not paying much attention to their surroundings.

"Let's make it count this time around." I handed a sizeable sum of euros to Akil.

I stood a few feet back as Akil spoke to the guard. I watched him slip the money to the guard via a friendly handshake. He then turned and motioned for me to follow.

We walked a few steps behind the guard. As he approached the other two guards near the gate, he said something and casually waved his hand to open the gate. The guards did as he said without so much as a break in their initial conversation, and we were officially in Cambodia.

"That went smoothly," I said.

"Here everyone can be bought. He'll split the take with those men."

At that point, our bus had long disappeared. "Surely there are other buses heading to Phnom Penh," I said, casting a sweeping gaze to the left and then right.

"More will be coming. We can wait… Shit!" A dark frown appeared on Akil's face.

"What?"

"That's why the driver left us." Akil said, pointing at the Cambodian immigration office.

I followed his line of sight and saw three young men standing near the entrance, their eyes scanning the area. They were all dressed in skinny jeans and fashionable button-downs with the sleeves rolled up, showing off their tattooed forearms.

"Those are KK members."

We crouched as we hurried over to an area where food vendors were set up. There were also two small tents housing a couple souvenir shops. We slipped into one of the tents and stood behind two circular racks—one filled with magnets and post cards, the other with cheap sunglasses.

"They know we're here. We can't risk waiting for another bus."

"Well, let's make it harder for them to find us." I bought T-shirts, sunglasses, and hats for both of us. We were the only shoppers in the stall, so we stayed put and changed.

"I think after last night, the gang sent men to watch the border," Akil said as he changed shirts. "They probably talked to every bus driver passing through."

I pulled a shirt over my blouse, slipped a ball cap over my head, and put on a pair of Ray Ban aviator knock-offs. "I don't see them."

"They're by the gate, talking to the guards."

Akil turned back to me. "The gang might be offering money to get people to talk. If that's true, the guards, the food vendors, everyone will give us up for a few dollars."

I took in the vendors around us, working tirelessly to eke out a meager living at best. I couldn't disagree with Akil. We moved out of the stall and behind it, heading away from the gate.

"There's a taxi there," I said but no sooner had those words left my mouth, two white women jumped inside it. I watched our ride drive off. "Damn!"

"It's okay. We'll pay someone to take us."

I looked back toward the guard gate; the three men had just passed through. "We better hurry."

"That car there." Akil pointed at a small Toyota parked next to a fruit vendor. In the driver's seat was an elderly man, maybe mid-fifties. A woman of similar age had just finished purchasing sliced pineapple and was opening the passenger door.

We hurried over to the vehicle. Akil knocked on the diver's window and motioned for him to lower it. I kept an eye on the gang members while Akil spoke to the man about a ride to Phnom Penh. I couldn't be sure if he understood everything Akil said, but smiling while shaking his head "no" was a pretty clear indicator he wanted nothing to do with us.

"Akil, those men are heading in our direction."

Akil continued to plead as he dropped a fistful of euros into the man's lap, but still he refused our proposition.

I removed more euros from my pocket and placed it directly inside the man's palm. "Please."

But he shook his hand free from mine and returned the bills. He then closed his window.

"The gang is getting closer," Akil said urgently.

I rapped my knuckles against the window, this time making eye contact with the woman. She only smiled and at me and then looked straight ahead.

Akil grabbed my arm. "Forget it. We'll find someone else."

"There is no one else," I said as I watched the elderly man put the car in gear.

"We have to go!" Akil said in an elevated voice.

I pulled more euros out of my pocket and slammed all of the bills against the window.

"Shit! I think they see us." Akil grabbed my arm and began to pull me away from the vehicle. "We have to go!"

The old man fumbled with the power button for his window and lowered it about three inches.

"Phnom Penh. Please," I said.

He let out a breath and looked as if he were reconsidering our offer until he saw Akil point to the three men heading toward our location. His eyes widened, and he quickly shook his head "no".

Chapter 30

Everyone can be bought. It was a matter of agreeing on a price. For the elderly couple, it was four hundred fifty euros. I turned the money over without argument, and we drove off just before the gang members reached us.

For the first thirty minutes or so, Akil tried to make small talk with the man and woman, but they didn't know much English aside from saying "okay" and a few other phrases. For the rest of the trip, everyone remained silent as the radio belted out a variety of Cambodian songs. Traffic on the highway was minimal and the man had a lead foot. The entire trip took two and a half hours. We even passed our bus on the way.

As we entered the outskirts of Phnom Penh, I waved more euros in front of the husband. "Thailand?"

"What are you doing?" Akil asked.

"I don't think heading to the bus terminal is a good idea. If the gang had the border covered, it's safe to assume they'll have some men waiting at the terminal. Convincing them to take us to the Thai border makes sense."

"We can't go there just yet," Akil whispered to me.

"Why not? That's where the nurse is."

"Bribing a Thai official doesn't always work."

"But you don't have a passport."

"I do. I just don't have it with me."

"What do you mean?" I asked, raising my voice.

"I rent a small apartment here. I'm sure I left it in there."

Akil quickly motioned for the husband to stop where we were. "We can get out here."

The husband pulled over and we quickly exited the vehicle onto a busy sidewalk, cluttered with street food vendors and hungry people pointing and waving money.

"This way," Akil said has he led me onto a small side street, away from the main thoroughfare.

I grabbed him by the shoulder and spun him around. "This is what I'm talking about. You continue to withhold information."

"I needed to be sure you would keep your word. If I tell you everything, you'll have no reason to help me."

"Do not presume to know what I might or might not do. And what makes you think that it's safe to go back to your apartment? Surely the gang has every location you could possibly be staked out, especially now that they know you were on your way to Phnom Penh."

Akil licked his lips. "We have no choice. I need that passport if I want to cross the Thai border. Maybe the gang doesn't think I'm that stupid to go back to my apartment," he said, looking back at me.

"But you are."

He shot me a look. "They might not have men there."

I sighed. "Your life," I said as I followed.

Akil led us through a series of backstreets until we reached a small market selling produce and seafood. We wove through the crowd of shoppers, passing wooden crates filled with mangos, papayas, dragon fruit, lychee, and other local fruit until we reached a stall that had a large group of people gathered in front of it. I didn't have to see to know what they were buying; my nose picked up the undeniable smells of rotting meat and sour milk. As we passed, I saw three women cutting open large, spiky durian fruit and packaging the custard-colored delicacy for the eager customers.

"There," Akil pointed across the street. "The building in the middle with the red door."

Across the street was a row of five-story apartment buildings. We moved around the durian stand and stood near another vendor doing brisk business with red, prickly rambutan fruit. We blended with the crowd and took a few minutes to survey the entrance.

"I don't see any of them," Akil said. "I think it's safe."

We hurried across the street, entered the building, and made our way up the stairs to the third floor. What I saw when Akil opened the door to his studio apartment wasn't encouraging. All of the dresser drawers were open and the contents strewn across the carpeted floor. The pillows on the sofa were sliced open, and the mattress from the bed was off kilter, revealing a torn box spring. The small flat-screen TV sitting on a desk had been smashed with a portable single-burner stove.

"Did you forget to pay the rent?" I asked, closing the door behind us.

"They were here looking for me and probably the money I owe them for the girl."

"And how much would that be?" I asked, thinking it might be easier to pay and be done with them.

"Two hundred thousand. American."

So much for that idea—it was a lot more than what I had on me.

"Do you think they found your passport?" I rested my hands on my hips and looked around.

"No," Akil said, smiling as he walked over to a small vent on the wall. He got down on all fours and peered through the grating. He clapped his hands together. "My passport is still there. You see, I'm not so stupid." He stood up, still smiling at me.

"What are you waiting for? Get your passport," I said as I eyed the peeling wallpaper above him.

"I need a coin to unscrew the grate."

I patted my pockets. "I don't have one on me."

"It's okay, I'm sure there's one here somewhere."

While Akil rummaged through the desk drawer, I kicked through a pile of old newspapers and unopened junk mail.

"Found one. You see, we have nothing to worry about."

"Until you have your passport in hand, let's refrain from celebrating."

Chapter 31

Shoppers shouted out orders for the purple mangosteen piled high in wooden crates, but the fruit vendor turned away and continued with his cell phone conversation.

From the moment Akil fled town, the KK gang had made the vendors at the market aware of their interest in him. They had a powerful presence and no one wanted to be seen as unhelpful, so the vendors remained vigilant for the first week or so, keeping watch on customers and the building across the street. But over time they had all given up and returned to the everyday hustle—all except Narith.

Narith turned away from the crowd and stuck a forefinger into his ear so he could hear the person on the phone more clearly. "Yes. I'm sure," he said, as he eyed an apartment window across the street.

He nodded eagerly as he spoke into his phone, even with customers walking away to purchase fruit from another vendor. Narith wasn't concerned about the lost business; he knew one day that foreigner would return to his apartment, and he would be the one to collect the large finder's fee.

◇◇◇

At the bus terminal, a white van pulled into a stall and six passengers exited. Privately run vans cost more, but they also travel faster than a bus. Mdivani was the last to exit the vehicle.

He made his way over to the arrival board and saw that the bus from Ho Chi Minh City had just arrived. He hurried over to the parking spot assigned it. The last of the passengers were debarking, but he didn't see Sei or Akil.

The bus driver was busy unloading luggage, and Mdivani tapped him on the shoulder. "Was this man on the bus?" he asked as he showed him a picture of Akil.

The bus driver ignored his question and returned to his work. Mdivani tapped him once more, held out fifty euros, and asked the same question.

The bus driver looked around briefly before snatching the bill. "He get off at border. Not come to Phnom Penh."

"There was a woman with him. Did she get off too?"

The driver nodded.

Mdivani wasn't expecting to hear that; he walked away a bit dumfounded. *What did I miss?* He mentally walked through the steps that led him to believe they were traveling to Phnom Penh. Perhaps he had over looked something but nothing stuck out. Everything pointed to Phnom Penh.

Fearing he had lost them, Mdivani returned to question the driver again, but upon his approach, he saw a group of men had surrounded him. The driver stood in a defensive position, hands out in front and appeared to be apologizing. Two of them were handling machetes, and they didn't look like farmers.

The men searched the bus and the remaining luggage with no protest from the passengers. If they were after money, the driver had a crisp fifty in his pocket he could have turned over and surely the passengers had money for the taking. One of the men continued to badger the driver, who continued to plead.

The more Mdivani observed, the more he believed this wasn't a shakedown. It was public, the men were spending too much time with the driver, and they didn't seem concerned about any of the other arriving buses. It was too coincidental to ignore that they happened to be interested in the bus that had just arrived from Ho Chi Minh City.

Mdivani wondered if this had to do with why Akil and Sei exited the bus at the border? Was someone else after Akil? Another assassin hired by the Wolf?

Before Mdivani could rationalize another thought, the man questioning the driver took a call on his cell phone. After hanging up, he quickly huddled the others and they hurried out of the station without so much as another look at the driver. *It's not him they're concerned with.* Mdivani's interest couldn't have been piqued any more by their quick departure. *Are we looking for the same person?*

Chapter 32

Akil's apartment also had a single window that looked out to a fire escape. A tattered curtain barely covered it. Just under it was the couch. I knelt on one of the cushions, and the springs gave way, forcing me to use my hands to steady myself. I moved the curtain enough to peek outside. Nothing appeared out of the ordinary. The street below had a steady flow of motorbikes, and the market across the street remained busy while locals trudged up and down the footpath.

I removed the souvenir shirt I had put on earlier, as well as the ball cap and shades, and fluttered the front of my blouse to cool myself. Aside from the mess, the heat in the room was noticeable from the moment we entered. Every breath was akin to opening a hot oven and inhaling deeply, but I refused to open the window. It might draw unnecessary attention.

"How long does it take to remove four screws?" I asked, turning back to Akil, who was lying prone on the floor with his shades still on.

"This coin keeps slipping, but I only have one more screw."

"Maybe removing the sunglasses might help."

He ignored my advice and continued to fiddle with the last screw. I thought it might be faster if I did it. Just as I started walking toward him, the sound of shattering glass erupted behind me.

Akil jerked up with bulging eyes. I spun around to find a machete clearing the glass from the windowsill.

"They've found us!" Akil shouted.

Within seconds, a young man climbed through the window, swinging a machete. I drew my knife, rushed forward, and slashed at his forearm. He let out a yelp and dropped his weapon. His cry of pain didn't last very long. The second pass of my knife tore open his neck.

I turned back to Akil, who lay frozen against the wall. "What are you waiting for? Open that grate!" I said, hurrying over to the front door and slamming the deadbolt into place.

By then two other men had made their way through the window. The first one in rushed toward Akil with his machete out front, but I cut him off with a leg kick to the side of his right knee, dislocating it, He dropped to his other knee, and I plunged my knife into the back of his neck. *Another one down.*

I spun around in time to avoid a downward slash from another machete. I was weaponless, as my knife was still lodged in the dead man's neck. The second attacker grinned as he realized my situation and followed with two more wild slashes. I sidestepped each one, but I was quickly nearing the wall behind me.

On his third attempt to slice me open, I caught his wrist, stepped in, and slammed an open palm straight into face, snapping his head back. I bent back his wrist to loosen his grip on the machete. He countered with a punch with his free hand. My forearm took the brunt of the hit, but he had grazed my cheek. I yanked him toward me, forcing him to step forward or fall on his face. At the same moment, I stepped in and slammed my forehead into his chest. A groan and a rush of air left his lips. My strike caved his boney chest, stunning him enough for me to wrestle the machete from his hand.

Still gripping his wrist, I swung the machete down, severing his arm at the elbow. He yelled and grabbed hold of his shortened limb, tucking it against his abdomen. I thought his eyes would pop out of their sockets when I threw his arm at him and shouted, "Catch!"

I spun around, hoping Akil wasn't still working on loosening that last screw. What I found was an empty room with the front door wide open.

Chapter 33

The second I stepped into the hall, another member from the KK gang nearly decapitated me. His machete lodged in the wall behind me. I reacted quickly, delivering a series of rapid punches to his face followed by a straight-leg kick to his midsection. That last move sent him flying backward into another man.

Up until then, the gang members I had faced were no more than five feet six or seven and rail thin. Not this one. He stood at least six feet tall and appeared to be carrying an extra twenty solid pounds for a man of his size. He had a shaved head and a large keloid scar that stretched from his left ear down to the corner of his mouth.

He pushed his fellow compatriot to the side and took a defensive stance, raising his arms and motioning for me to come at him. I wasn't afraid, but I also wasn't stupid enough to engage in a straight-up fistfight. I moved back to where the machete was stuck in the wall, planted a foot for leverage, and yanked the blade free.

He laughed and then bounced, surprisingly light, from foot to foot as he grabbed his pants about mid-thigh and yanked them up a bit.

We were separated by roughly twenty feet. I spun the machete in my hand to get a feel for the weight of the blade versus the handle.

This move caused him to laugh. "Come on, Kung Fu master," he said with a heavy accent as he readied himself for my attack.

I moved forward, but stopped after one step—the machete didn't. The steel blade rotated end over end rapidly, slicing through the air. *Thunk!*

Bull's eye. The blade had lodged itself in his forehead at an angle almost perpendicular with his nose. A red river appeared, splitting at the bridge of his nose and creating an upside down Y that continued down the sides of his face.

He remained frozen in his defensive position; he hadn't budged, not even a smidgen. He wasn't looking at me; his eyes were crossed inward, focused on the wooden handle. For a second, I wasn't quite sure if I had done as much damage as I thought I had. The other KK member stood still, mouth agape.

Slowly his lips widened into a smile and his shoulders bobbed as a low laugh sputtered to life. He grabbed hold of the handle with both hands and breathed forceful breaths through a clenched jaw. He pushed up on the handle and then down. Up, down. Up, down. Up, down. He continued to ease the blade out of his head. I swore I heard his skull crackle—time to exit.

I sprinted up the stairs. I was sure Akil had headed for

the roof.

After the fifth floor, the stairs continued to an open doorway leading to the rooftop. It was mostly flat save for a few foot-and-a-half-tall air vents and a couple of water reservoirs. There was no place to hide, not even behind the large satellite dishes.

I ran the only way that made sense: toward the far end of the roof. Just as I cleared the water tanks, I spotted Akil on the roof of the next building. The buildings were separated by no more than three feet at the most, and sometimes they were so close, crossing from building to building was as easy as stretching a step.

"Akil!" I called out.

He glanced back but didn't slow.

I picked up the pace, skirting the air vents along the way. "Akil, stop now!"

Each time I called out, he ignored me. My fists tightened and my nails cut into my palm as I pumped my arms. I had risked my life back at his apartment to save him, only to discover he had viewed that as an opportunity to run. Pathetic.

Akil wasn't very athletic, and he wasn't very fast. Two-foot-high walls signaled the edge of each building. He slowed each time to climb over, while I hurdled them. He was about seventy-five feet from me when he suddenly dropped out of sight. It was only when I got there that I understood why.

Chapter 34

Mdivani stuck with the gang of men when they left the bus terminal, remaining about thirty yards behind them until they reached an outdoor market, where he closed the distance as they made their way through the maze of produce stands. They stopped at one selling mangosteen and talked to a middle-aged male vendor with shifty eyes and a swiveling head. The vendor's lips moved rapidly, and he punctuated his words with repeated jabs at the apartment building opposite the market. *That's where Akil's hiding.*

Up until he arrived in Vietnam, Mdivani wasn't hired to execute a target. His orders were to watch Sei and report her actions to the Wolf. But that all changed right before he left France. The Wolf had given him permission to act on Akil's contract.

Mdivani wasn't picky about how he completed his contracts. His only concern was that he did what was required to receive payment. If his hunch was right, that these men were looking for Akil and had found him, why not let them do the dirty work? Mdivani didn't have an ego. All he needed to do was provide a picture of Akil's body for proof, and he would collect payment. If these men had other plans, then he would act appropriately at that time. For now he was content to wait and see how the show played out.

He purchased a bag of cherry-red, rose apples and took a seat on a wooden crate. From there, he watched three men climb up the fire escape to a third-floor apartment. Two remained outside guarding the entrance while two more entered the building.

As soon as the three on the fire escape entered the apartment, he heard yelling and then a commotion. He wasn't moved by it nor were the people shopping around him. He took a bite from an apple, glanced at his watch, and wondered how long it would take. He wondered very little about what would happen to Sei.

It didn't take long for the noise inside the apartment to subside. *Did she protect her investment?* A vendor near him shouted and pointed at the building. Mdivani looked up and saw Akil running along the rooftop.

He quickly swallowed the mouthful of apple, tossed the bag of remaining fruit at the feet of an elderly woman begging for change, and gave chase from the sidewalk below. He wasn't worried about the target getting away. Eventually Akil would run out of rooftop.

While skirting shoppers, parked motorbikes, and few street dogs, Mdivani heard a familiar voice call Akil's name. He scanned the rooftops and spotted Sei not far behind Akil. He now had an answer to his earlier question.

With Sei back in play, Mdivani could no longer sit

back and enjoy the show, especially now that he also noticed two of the men he saw earlier pursuing Sei. He kept his eyes focused on Akil as he traversed the rooftops of three buildings until he dropped from sight.

Chapter 35

When I reached the spot where Akil had disappeared, I realized he had dropped down into the patio of an apartment. A crisscross of clothing drying on lines covered most of the area. I slipped between them and landed softly on my feet, next to a few potted jade plants. An old lady sat quietly on a small stool in front of me. She had pink curlers in her hair and wore an old yellow-and-white-checkered housedress. She puffed away on a small cigar as she flashed me a toothless smile. She seemed to be enjoying the action unfolding before her and pointed to the door leading into the apartment. I nodded politely and ran past her.

I hand-vaulted over a table and two chairs and headed out the front door of the apartment. I glanced in both directions of the hallway, looking for the stairwell. It was to my left. I hurried down to the fourth floor. That was where I spotted Akil at the far end of the hallway. He was hanging halfway out of an open window.

"Akil, stop!"

Once again he ignored me and disappeared from view.

I stuck my head out of the window and saw him climbing down a vine-covered trellis that led to a tiny walkway about five-feet wide. To the right was the road. To the left, the passage continued for about twenty feet and then hooked right and disappeared from my view. I swung my right leg over the windowsill and eased myself out, hoping the trellis would hold us both.

Mdivani entered the building he last saw Akil running on top of and headed up the stairs. He removed his Beretta from the rear of his waistband and screwed on a sound suppressor he kept in his knapsack. Up the stairs he climbed, peeking up the center of the stairwell, expecting to see Akil making his way down. He didn't, nor did he hear the clomping of footsteps on the stairs. Either Akil had stopped somewhere or he found another exit out of the building.

When Mdivani reached the second floor, he stepped into the hallway and looked left and right. Empty and quiet. He continued up and did the same on the third floor. When he reached the fourth floor, it was also empty and quiet like the other floors except the window at the far end was open. *I've got you now.*

He moved quickly down the hall, holding the Beretta out in front. When he was a few feet away from the window, he slowed and looked over his shoulder. He still hadn't seen Sei.

"Akil, stop!" I shouted.

I had closed the gap between us. He was about a foot and a half away. If I didn't still need information from him, I would have released my grip, dropped down, and allowed him to cushion my fall to the ground.

He had just passed the second floor window and could jump from his position, but he would still risk breaking an ankle if he didn't land right. Not ideal since the Asian Hulk and his sidekick were chasing me on the roof.

I did my best to pick up my pace so I could position myself alongside Akil. Once there, I would pull him off the trellis and down to the pavement. The fall would be manageable. But Akil, surprisingly kept his distance. At any second I expected him to let go and fall to the ground.

I hadn't seen the two gang members since I entered the building but wasn't convinced I had lost them. I kept looking up, expecting to see them leaning out the window. They weren't, but a Caucasian man aiming a gun was.

The vines were thick and unruly, blocking most of Mdivani's sightline toward Akil. Sei was just to Akil's left. He leaned out as far as he could and aimed his weapon, positioning the sights of his Beretta at the top of Akil's head. Behind him, he could hear footsteps stomping toward him, but he couldn't take his eyes off Akil. Not just yet.

A split second later, Mdivani fired and watched Akil fall to the pavement and roll backward under the awning of the neighboring building.

Mdivani then spun to face whomever it was he had heard running toward him. It was the two men who had been chasing Sei on the roof. He wasn't sure what their intentions were or why they were approaching him so aggressively, but Mdivani wasn't about to wait and find out.

He fired a round straight into the forehead of the first man running toward him. His legs buckled, and he collapsed to the floor in a dead heap. The larger man behind him had a nasty wound on his forehead, and blood covered his entire face. Even though his friend had just taken a hot slug, he didn't slow his approach. In fact, he picked up his pace.

Mdivani pulled the trigger, and the bullet struck the man in his cheek but didn't seem to have much effect. Mdivani fired two rounds into the man's chest, and this time the giant fell to the floor. When he leaned back out the window, Sei was gone.

Chapter 36

I ran behind Akil, keeping my hand firmly pressed against his back so he wouldn't slow. The assassin's bullet had just missed him. Had he not jumped when I told him to, he most likely would be lying dead on the pavement.

However, what I found most troubling was that the assassin had tracked us to Phnom Penh and with pinpoint accuracy. *He may not be a great shot but if he keeps finding us, it's only a matter of time before his bullets find their mark.* He had already missed Akil twice. Or in other words, that was twice luck had favored Akil.

After we rounded the initial corner, the walkway ended in a T intersection. "Left," I said.

We turned and ran fifteen feet to another T intersection. "Which way?" Akil shouted.

"Right."

The maze of passageways wound between buildings and through enclosed courtyards. When I thought we were far enough from the assassin, I grabbed hold of Aki's collar and yanked him back to a stop. I shoved him against the building and kept both hands fastened tightly around his shirt.

"I don't care what information you have. If you ever run from me again, I will be the one who ends your life. Am I clear?"

Akil sort of nodded as he looked me over. "Where's your knife?" he asked.

I leaned in, my face inches from his. "I don't need a knife. Remember that."

A woman screamed in the far distance, prompting Akil to look in that direction. "Okay," he huffed. "Let go of me."

We continued running through the narrow passageway until we were a good distance away from that building.

"Who was shooting at me?" he asked, looking back over his shoulder.

"I believe it's the same person that tried to shoot you in Ho Chi Minh."

"I thought you said we lost him."

"We did. He found us again."

He shook his head. "How? How did he know we would be there?"

"I believe he's a tracker."

"A what?"

"He finds people. He appears to be exceptional at his job. The up side is he's not great at killing."

Akil crinkled his brow before turning away.

"I know what he looks like. It'll be harder for him to approach us." I placed my hand on Akil's back to hurry him.

"Are you sure?" he asked with a dismissive breath. "You were wrong the first time."

"Akil, you have two people who want to see you dead. Don't make it three."

Chapter 37

Mdivani exited the building and ran into the passageway. He expected to find Akil dead, but instead he found nothing. *I thought I got him.* Given that Sei was also MIA, he assumed there were still together and running. He followed the walkway to where it hooked to the right and ran into a T intersection. He looked right and the passageway continued straight back out to the road. He looked left and saw another T intersection.

There was a shop to the left of him selling woven baskets of various sizes. Just outside the entrance an elderly man sat on a folding chair fashioned out of bamboo. He had deep weathered lines that cut into his dark-skinned face and inhaled repeatedly on a hand-rolled cigarette.

Mdivani removed his phone from his pants pocket and showed a picture of Akil to the old man. "You see?" he asked, pointing in both directions of the passageway. "Where?"

The man said nothing and took another short pull.

Mdivani let out a loud breath and pocketed his phone before heading toward the T intersection. Off in the distance, he could hear sirens. He wondered if the bodies had been found. To the left was an old lady sweeping the entrance area to her building. Mdivani showed her the photo. "You see?" he asked, pointing at his phone.

The woman steadied his hand and leaned in closer. She then stabbed her fingers at the menu, closing the picture and revealing a grid of icon applications on the phone. She swiped through them before asking how much for the phone.

"What?"

"How much phone?"

Mdivani jerked his hand out of her grasp and nearly knocked the fragile woman to the ground with his arm as he moved around her. He could still hear her cursing even after he had disappeared from her view. The wail of sirens had become increasingly louder, confirming his earlier assumption. Soon the area would be crawling with police. He continued showing the photo to every person he passed but had no luck. Sei and Akil had vanished without anyone seeing them. Mdivani wasn't deterred. Everyone left a trail.

Chapter 38

We continued moving until we reached a quiet, residential part of the city. We had done our best to throw the assassin off of our trail by doubling back, cutting through restaurants and shops, and never looking anyone directly in the eyes.

I utilized every tactic I had learned through my training as a young teen. Infiltration was where I excelled. To me, that was a skill worth mastering, one that gave me an undeniable advantage in my profession. During my training, I focused on developing my ability to get in and out of any sort of environment without anyone knowing. I wanted to be a ghost.

Still, I was troubled by the fact that this particular assassin was able to locate us not once but twice. Very few people had the skills needed to find me, even trained assassins. Most of them focused on honing their ability to kill. While important, it did them no good if they couldn't find the mark or figure out how to get close enough to deliver a fatal blow. But there was a subset of assassins I knew of who excelled at tracking. The assassin after Akil was obviously one of them.

I'd come across a few of these individuals in my
lifetime. There were two who lived within my clan while
growing up. They were the best I'd ever seen in that
particular skill set, but I had seen this assassin's face and I
didn't recognize him. I had to be careful. I could easily put
Akil and myself into a position I may not be able to save us.
Well, him.

I had to wonder if this assassin had been tracking me in
Paris. If so, was he working with the assassin who killed
Feki and Yesmine? Why couldn't he complete the contract
himself? I thought it odd. Why would the Wolf want to keep
tabs on me? Was I closer to locating him than I thought? Is
that why he ordered the deaths of everyone involved with
the birth of my child?

I tried to put myself in his shoes. Why would I want to
keep tabs on my adversary? What purpose or interest would
that serve beyond protection? Then I had a moment of
clarity.

He's using me to find them.

Clever. I had to give him that. Putting a tracker assassin
on me only helped increase the odds of him eliminating
everyone. I'd already led him to Akil, and I could very well
lead him to the nurse in Thailand. I had to lose him or
eliminate him. Neither option would be easy.

One thing was certain: I needed to keep Akil alive until
we reached the Thai border. After that, the assassin could
have his way with him. The situation was the same with the

nurse; as soon as I learned what information she had about my daughter or the Wolf, she would cease to be a person of interest to me.

As far as I was concerned, all of these individuals were involved in the kidnapping of my daughter. I felt no guilt. These people were already marked. The Wolf wouldn't stop until he knew they were all dead. It wasn't my duty to keep them alive, I just needed to stay far enough ahead of the tracker.

"Hold up," I said as we passed a small gothic church. There was a Latin inscription carved into the stone header above the entrance and a poorly maintained stained-glass portrait above that.

"What?" he asked.

"We need to determine our next steps forward."

I grabbed the weathered metal handle of one of the wooden doors. Both were warped due to age and humidity, but nothing a hard tug couldn't solve. I peeked inside. It took a moment for my eyes to adjust to the dim candlelight inside the old building. The air inside was noticeably cooler and fragrant with burning incense. I counted five rows of pews with an aisle down the middle. Each one sat four or five people comfortably—not a big congregation. But what was most important was that the church was empty.

"Come on," I said, holding the door open. "This place will do."

"You plan to ask your god for help?"

"No, but I would advise you to reach out to yours."

We sat on the left side, in the third pew from the front. "After what happened, the bus terminal won't work," I said. "The assassin might even be heading there. We'll need to find other transport to Thailand."

Akil crossed a leg over the other and then scratched at his chin until a light in his head seemed to click on. "I got it," he said, snapping his fingers.

He removed his cell phone from his fanny bag and dialed a number. He spoke in Tunisian with the person on the other end. The conversation started off cordial, but by the time he ended the call, it had turned into a shouting match.

"Okay, it's settled," he said tucking his phone away. "I have a friend who can help us."

"Really?" I pulled my head back and raised an eyebrow. "It sounded as if he wanted nothing to do with you."

Akil waved me off. "It's always like this between us."

"Can you trust him? You keep saying everyone here can be bought. What makes you so sure he isn't dreaming of collecting a finder's fee for your head?"

"Don't worry—we're related from my mother's sister's husband's side. It'll be okay."

I let out a breath. "Fine. Is he meeting us here?"

He shook his head. "We will meet him in one hour. Not far from here, at the Russian Market."

Chapter 39

Ponleak was second in command and a cofounder of the Khmer Kings. He and another man, Li'l Cambo, were known as Cambodian throwbacks—citizens who immigrated to America during the seventies and eighties but were then deported later in life.

Both had parents who didn't follow through with obtaining citizenship for themselves or their children after arriving in the States. As teens, they joined up with the Asian Assault Force, a Cambodian gang located in Long Beach, California. They were arrested and convicted for a series of burglaries shortly after they both turned twenty-one.

After serving five-year prison terms in Los Angeles County State Prison both men were promptly deported back to Cambodia with no chance of ever legally returning to the States. With no real future ahead of them and gang life being the only thing they knew, they started the Khmer Kings gang.

"Ponleak!" the voice called out, followed by two thumps against the bedroom door. "Get up."

Ponleak rolled over onto his back and opened his eyes.

The sun shining through the sheer curtains stung and forced him to squint. He licked his lips and tasted the sour still residing inside his mouth from last night's intoxicating revelry.

He sat up and swung his feet over the side of the bed and rubbed the crust from his eyes.

"Did you hear me?" the voice outside continued.

Ponleak managed a hoarse reply. "I heard you." He grabbed the pack of Marlboros off the bedside table, tapped out a cigarette and lit it. He took a long pull, and the nicotine rush quickly breathed life back into his senses. He sat for another minute before exiting his bedroom and shuffling barefoot to the kitchen.

"So glad you could join me," Li'l Cambo said, looking up. He was sitting at the kitchen table counting a massive pile of American dollars. There was also a Colt .45 handgun laying on the glass tabletop.

The two shared a four-bedroom, three-bath villa with a swimming pool and other luxury amenities. They agreed when they formed the gang that living together and sharing everything equally would keep their relationship strong and free from pettiness.

"Man, you look like shit." Li'l Cambo let out a hearty laugh as his friend took a seat next to him.

Ponleak was wearing white boxers and an undershirt. His hair was in a lopsided faux-hawk. He scratched his armpit as he sucked on the cigarette.

Li'l Cambo was the fitter of the two, sticking to a strict daily regimen at the gym. Since their return to Cambodia, he had managed to pack twenty pounds of muscle onto his five-foot-seven-inch frame. Ponleak chose to be at peace with his beer belly. It really wasn't very big and stood out only because the rest of his frame was thin.

"Too much last night," Ponleak grunted. "What's all this?"

"While you were out getting hammered, the card game got hit hard last night. A couple of lucky players nearly cleaned us out. I have to replenish the reserves for tonight."

Trafficking young girls wasn't the gang's only source of income. They also had their hands in hosting pop-up gambling dens, collecting protection money from vendors in a few of the outdoor markets, and counterfeiting—mostly athletic shoes. Knockoff sneakers sold well to the wannabes who couldn't afford the hundred-to-two-hundred price tags on the real goods. This was the area where Ponleak really wanted to steer the gang's interest. Child prostitution was a niche market and high risk. Counterfeiting the hottest shoe brands was a safer bet and had widespread appeal. In the long run, it would rake in more profits. Ponleak tapped ash into an empty paper cup before taking another pull.

"After I have to go to Siem Reap to take care of that thing," Li'l Cambo continued.

"You want me to come?" Ponleak asked, raising an eyebrow.

A few weeks ago, the gang had set up a small gambling den there, but it wasn't without its problems. Both suspected the man they hired to manage the operation was skimming from the profits. Li'l Cambo intended to find out once and for all if this was the truth.

"No. One of us should stay here. I'll take Atith and Chea with me. If he's cheating us, I'll take care of it." Li'l Cambo nodded at the handgun.

Most of the members in the gang utilized knives or machetes as their weapons of choice for conducting business. Intimidation and a beating went a long way in keeping people in line. Li'l Cambo thought otherwise. He liked kneeling a man down, pressing the barrel of a gun against the back of his head, and pulling the trigger—a habit he had brought back after serving as an enforcer for the AAF gang in Long Beach, California.

Just then, Ponleak's cell phone rang. "What? Wait. Slow down. Tell me everything. I see... Uh-huh. How many are hurt? Dead? I told you not to do anything without me. No, I'll meet you there." He frowned at the phone as he disconnected.

"What's up?" Li'l Cambo asked.

"That was Acharya. Akil is back in town and he brought protection—a woman." Ponleak went on to explain what had happened at Akil's apartment.

"Bora and Devi are dead? Who is this bitch? I'm coming with you." Li'l Cambo grabbed the Colt off the table.

"No!" Ponleak placed a hand on Li'l Cambo's arm. "I need to take care of this. I need to be the one who deals with Akil. Chivy deserves that much." His eyes were filled with determined vengeance.

Two years earlier, Ponleak had met Chivy when her mother was in the process of selling the seven-year-old to one of the many brothels in Svay Pak. He was making a deal with the owner for another matter when he caught sight of the little girl's large brown eyes and infectious smile. He'd convinced the mother not to sell her.

In exchange, Ponleak supported the family, paid for Chivy's schooling, and covered other unexpected expenses. He had loved her like she was his own child. Ponleak had no sexual interest in children and shielded her from that world as best as he could.

One night, Ponleak asked Akil to drive Chivy back home because gang business had come up unexpectedly. The following day, Chivy's mother called asking where she was. When Ponleak questioned Akil, he insisted he had dropped the girl off a few blocks away from her home because she wanted to visit a friend.

A few days later, the police found Chivy's bloated body tangled in the mangroves of the Mekong River. She had suffered multiple contusions to her face and had signs of forced vaginal and anal entry, but ultimately a local medical examiner named asphyxiation as the cause of death.

When Ponleak summoned Akil to the villa for further explanations, he never showed. He never returned calls. He had disappeared. But Ponleak wasn't one to forget.

"She was a good girl," Li'l Cambo said, his eyes softened for a moment. They narrowed as he continued. "And if Akil's responsible for killing our men..."

"Don't worry, I will take care of it. They should have called me the minute they knew he was back in Cambodia. This is what I get for relying on them to locate Akil instead of handling it myself. Stupid fuckers tried to be heroes again and grab him. They already screwed up in Ho Chi Minh."

"I know you need to take care of this yourself," Li'l Cambo said. "But if you want me to help…" He gave Ponleak a strong pat on the shoulder.

Ponleak appreciated his friend's offer but this was his fight. He had to be the one to deal with Akil.

Chapter 40

Sei was much better than Mdivani had anticipated. After losing them in the passageway, he determined that the bus terminal would be his best shot at picking up their trail. It was the most obvious of places, at least to him, and most likely to Sei. It was clear they hadn't come to Phnom Penh to meet with someone. They needed something in that apartment, and it wasn't important to Sei. If it were, Akil would have handed it over, and they would have separated. But that wasn't the case.

She had chased after him on the rooftop, and when she caught him, there were no consequences. Instead, she helped him again when they were climbing down the trellis. She still needed Akil, and Mdivani still had a chance to prevent her from getting whatever it was.

The only other variable Mdivani couldn't quite determine was whether they still had business to conduct in Phnom Penh or were they on their way out? All he could surmise was that if they were leaving, they would do so right away. Covering the bus terminal was his only option at the moment.

After arriving at the terminal, Mdivani conducted a

quick walkthrough but didn't see the two. He made note of
the bus schedule and the destinations of the departing buses:
Siem Reap, Ho Chi Minh City, Thailand, Vientiane, Hanoi
were the major destinations. There were a number of places
they could go within Cambodia but Mdivani's gut told him
they would leave the country.

He found an area where he could remain out of sight
but still have an unobstructed view of the terminal entrance
and ticket windows. He took a seat in a blue molded-plastic
chair that was anchored to five others and surveyed the area.
Travelers were lined up at the ticket booths to purchase
tickets. The food carts had brisk business; even the lone
restaurant serving a combination of American and
Cambodian food—burgers and stir-fry—had its tables
filled. Suitcase after suitcase wheeled by in front of him.
Mdivani put on a pair of imitation Ray Ban Wayfarers he
picked up in Vietnam and folded his hands on his lap,
content to play the role of a tourist.

It wasn't long before a group of men walked through
the entrance. Gauging from their urban street attire and
tattooed arms, Mdivani pegged them as associates of the
men who were chasing Akil earlier. *Reinforcements?* Were
they also expecting Akil to leave Phnom Penh or were they
covering all their bases?

He took a sip of the fresh-pressed pomegranate juice he
had purchased from the vendor next to him. It was cool and
refreshing with the right amount of tart. The handle of the

Beretta he had hidden in the waistband of his pants dug into his back, prompting him to shift in his chair more often then he would have liked.

To pass the time, he decided to update his employer. This was not something he was particularly looking forward to, given there was a fifty-fifty chance he had lost Sei and Akil. He removed his cell phone from his pants pocket and opened a messenger application.

After a few seconds, Mdivani received a response from Vasili Ivanovich. All communications went through him. No one spoke directly to the Wolf. He spent the next few minutes bringing Ivanovich up to speed on everything that had taken place since his arrival in Vietnam. He grimaced slightly when having to mention that two opportunities to kill Akil had failed. Still, Ivanovich praised the assassin's ability to track them as far as he had.

Mdivani: Akil hasn't told her everything he knows.

Ivanovich: How can you be sure of this?

Mdivani: She is still with him. I believe he's taking her to someone. Could be one of the other targets.

Ivanovich: These other men after Akil, who are they?

Mdivani: I'm not sure. A local gang, maybe. They've made two attempts to catch Akil. They're capable of more.

Ivanovich: You must pick up the trail. You cannot lose them.

Mdivani: Understood.

Ivanovich: I have new orders from the Wolf. Do not kill Akil and make sure no one else does either.

Mdivani blinked his eyes and reread the text. He couldn't understand why his directives had changed, again. First, he wasn't allowed to act on any open contracts, then he was told he could have Akil's contract, and now that offer was being rescinded. He couldn't help but think that perhaps his ability had come into question.

Mdivani: Why am I losing the contract? I can get him. Believe me.
Ivanovich: You are mistaking our intentions. If Akil is leading Sei to another target, you can kill that one as well. This is the Wolf's wish.
Mdivani: What about the girl?
Ivanovich: Your orders on her have not changed. She is not to be harmed.

Mdivani lowered his phone as he came to grips with his new mission. Not only was Sei keeping Akil alive, it was now his job to do so as well.

Chapter 41

We remained in the quiet sanctuary a bit longer, until people filed in for afternoon mass. According to Akil, the Russian Market was nearby, maybe a twenty-minute walk from the church. On the way over there, I inquired again about the person we were meeting.

"His name is Yanick Kanzari. He's Tunisian. Nothing to worry about," Akil said rather casually, walking with both hands buried in his pants pockets.

"What is he doing in Cambodia?"

"Enjoying the warm weather and fresh fruit."

I raised an eyebrow. "You're doing it again. Making me want to hurt you."

Akil let out exaggerated breath. "I pay him to help me bring the girls to the border. That's it."

Knowing we were seeking help from another sex trafficker wasn't something I wanted to hear. I kept thinking about my own daughter. How would I feel if the sex trade wrapped its ugly tentacles around her? It sickened me. Every month, thousands of girls were forced into that business. They were kept as slaves, used until their value was depleted, and then discarded like trash. It seemed there was no stopping it.

"How much farther?" I barked.

"We're almost there. A few blocks," Akil answered.

"When we meet Yanick, you are not to repeat anything I've told you or tell him anything about what happened at the clinic. Is that understood?"

Akil nodded but refrained from looking at me.

I tried to keep the information I relayed about my situation and myself to a minimum, only what was needed to jar his memory. I didn't like exposing my life to others, let alone to those I despised.

The Russian Market was a large indoor market that slightly resembled the Grand Bazaar in Istanbul. There were stalls selling oriental rugs stacked ten-feet high, hanging glass lanterns in an array of colors, and handmade copperware. There were the usual suspects selling clothing, handbags, makeup, jewelry, and souvenirs.

The lanes were fairly narrow, heavy with heat and the pungent body odor of tightly packed shoppers rubbing shoulders. We pressed forward to a small stall near the rear of the market, one selling roasted coffee beans.

"This is Yanick's shop," Akil said.

Large glass jars lined the front of the stall, each filled to the brim with various shades of coffee beans. Handwritten signs promoted the popular dung-harvested coffee. It seemed every country had a version of beans that were plucked from excrement of the civet cat. Some experimented with other animals. In Thailand, they had Black Ivory coffee, beans gathered from elephant droppings. My guess was that ninety percent of that shitty coffee wasn't authentic.

Yanick and Akil kissed each other on the cheek twice before placing a hand over their chest. "*As-salam alaykum,*" Akil said.

"*Wa alaykum e-salam,*" Yanick replied.

"Yanick, this is Sei, the woman I told you about."

Yanick gave me a polite nod of his head.

"Is there someplace we can speak privately?" Akil asked.

"Yes, of course."

Yanick didn't look very different from Akil. He stood about the same height and appeared to be in the same age range. He had longer hair, and his skin color was a little darker. He also had a noticeably crooked hook nose. It had been broken on more than one occasion. He dressed better, wearing a light blue, long-sleeve button-down, black slacks, and leather shoes. Neither the heat nor the humidity seemed to bother him. In fact, I had noticed that it never bothered Akil either.

At the rear of his shop, we walked through a narrow doorway into a small storage area. We were blocked from sight by a beaded curtain across the opening. No sooner had we entered the space than Yanick stopped with the pleasantries.

"Akil, you are crazy to have come back here. The KK have not forgotten about you."

"My friend, everything is okay."

"Okay?" A disturbing frown covered Yanick's face. "Do they know you are back in town?"

Akil glanced briefly at me. That was enough to answer Yanick's question. He dropped his head into his palm and mumbled a few Tunisian words.

A moment later, Yanick looked up at us. "I'm sorry, but I can't be a part of this. I cannot help you. Both of you must leave now," he said, pointing at the doorway.

I grabbed hold of his hand and twisted it down and back, which caused Yanick to bend at the waist and twist his torso to alleviate the pain. "Ow, ow," he whined.

"We're not leaving, and you will help us. Is that understood?"

"Yes, yes, let go."

Chapter 42

Shortly after I made it clear to Yanick on what it was he would be doing, he closed his shop for the day and escorted us back to his apartment.

"Yanick, how sure are you the gang isn't watching your place?"

He looked at me and then answered. "You're forcing me to do something I don't want to do. What do you think?"

I had just started to protest when Akil interjected.

"It's okay, Sei. Yanick never met anyone from the gang. They don't know him. This is exactly why I didn't introduce you to them, Yanick. Aren't you happy I kept you away?"

"No, it's you who is happy you kept me away. Now you have a safe place to invite yourself to."

We stayed off the main roads and stuck to smaller backstreets, utilizing the passageways that ran between buildings to reach Yanick's place. He lived in a small one-bedroom apartment on the first floor of what appeared to be a family home.

His apartment had an open design and looked homey. It contained one brown fabric sofa with two matching chairs and a wooden coffee table. There were a few newspapers sitting on top of it, along with an empty coffee mug. Off to the side was a tiny kitchen consisting of a short countertop with a two-burner range and a sink. A row of cabinets hung above it. An open doorway led to his bedroom—inside I saw a single mattress on the floor and a four-drawer dresser.

"How long have you lived in Phnom Penh?" I asked as I walked across the room toward a shelf adhered to a wall. On top of it were a few framed pictures of what looked like family.

"Ten years," he answered. "I've been in this apartment for eight. Families here often rent out a floor or a room in their homes for extra income. It's small, but it's enough for me."

"What about your family?"

"They're back in Tunisia."

"You came here alone?"

This time Yanick hesitated before answering. "Yes."

I wasn't sure if he was lying or annoyed with my questions. I wasn't interested in small talk; I just wanted a better handle on his situation in Phnom Penh. I didn't trust Akil, and there was absolutely no reason to trust Yanick.

"Please, sit," Yanick said, pointing at the two chairs. "I'll fix us some tea." He filled a kettle with water and put it on the stove.

I continued to stand while Akil ignored Yanick and headed for the small fridge. "Do you have anything to eat?"

Yanick answered in his native language, prompting Akil to look back at me. "Hungry? Yes? I'll fix us something to eat."

I was a bit surprised at the offer of a meal and tea. I didn't think either man had a desire to do anything for me unless they were being forced, in the case of Yanick, or they had something to gain—Akil. There was also the uneasiness I felt with staying in one place too long. It made one an easier target.

With both of their backs facing me, they busied themselves. Akil chopped vegetables: squash, onions, tomatoes, garlic and a few other items I couldn't quite see. Into a pot it went. Yanick removed a bag from the fridge filled with chicken legs and washed them under running water. Into the pot it went. While preparing the meal they spoke with each other in hushed tones. I heard enough to recognize they were speaking Tunisian. I peeked out a window and then walked into Yanick's bedroom, where there was another window.

"This woman is crazy," Yanick said. "Why is she with you?"

"She is saving my life right now," Akil said as he cut a red onion into quarters. "She can kill. She's a professional."

"But who is she? Why does she want to help you?"

"It has to do with something that took place over two years ago." He told Yanick about his job at the clinic in Paris and what had happened.

"You helped kidnap that woman's baby?"

"No. I had no idea that had happened until she told me. She's searching for the man responsible."

"And you know this man?"

"I know somebody who might. If she gets me to Thailand, I'll tell her. This is our agreement."

"You think she'll keep her end of the deal?"

"Yes. She has kept me safe from the gang and some other man."

"Another man? You have someone—"

"What are you two talking about?" I asked when I returned.

Both men turned their heads. "We're talking about how to get to the border," Akil answered, brushing his hands.

"Do tell me what plan you two have devised."

"In a minute. I have to go the bathroom," Akil said.

"The food will be done in thirty minutes," Yanick said as he wiped his hands with a washcloth. "It needs to simmer." He then brought three cups filled with tea over to the coffee table and placed them on the table.

Yanick and I sipped our tea quietly until Akil returned.

He clapped his hands together and rubbed them as he took a seat. "Yanick, did you tell her the plan?

He perked up and struggled to speak. "I, I, um, well... Did we agree on a plan? I wasn't sure."

The question had been thrown back to Akil, who now had a case of the mumbles. Clearly they weren't discussing ways to travel to the border.

"I won't ask the question again. One of you had better start making sense." I placed my cup on the table before leaning back and crossing a leg over the other.

Yanick shifted in his seat. "I can drive us to the border, but it will be better if we left at night. The cover of dark will help."

I glanced at my watch—it was a half past three. I didn't like the idea of remaining in this place for that long. "I think we should move as soon as we can. The longer we stay here, the greater the chance we'll be discovered."

Yanick bounced both of his legs as he looked at Akil. "The KK are everywhere. Tell her, Akil."

"Maybe we can wait until sunset. It's only a couple of hours. Plus, we have a meal." He motioned with his head to the large pot on the stovetop.

"What sort of transport do you have?" I asked Yanick.

"I have a small car, but we can all fit."

"Is it reliable?" I asked, raising my eyebrows.

Yanick nodded quickly. "Yes, yes."

"Akil, will we have problems crossing over into

Thailand?" I asked.

"None at all," he said. "I have my passport. We will cross like tourist. No visa is needed for a French passport. And your passport is?"

"Of no concern to you," I said.

Yanick slapped his hands against his thighs and stood. "Let me check on the food."

He remained at the counter tending to the pot, while Akil and I continued to sip our tea. I let out a yawn. It surprised me but I guessed the constant running had begun to catch up with me.

"You okay? You want to lie down?" Akil asked, tilting his head.

"I'm fine." The truth was I suddenly felt sleepy. I wanted nothing more than to close my eyes for a bit. I'd never had a problem fighting off a drowsy spell and didn't think I would then, even if it hit me bit harder than usual.

Akil continued to stare at me with prominent lines across his forehead.

"What?" I asked.

"You fell asleep. You sure you don't want to lie down?"

"What are you talking about? I haven't taken my eyes off you."

"No, your eyes were closed."

Chapter 43

Akil knelt next to Sei's chair and shook her arm gently. "Sei, Sei!"

There was no response from her. She sat motionless with her head resting on her shoulder.

"Yanick, what did you do?"

"What are you talking about?" Yanick shrugged and then removed three bowls from the cabinet. Akil tried again to wake Sei; this time she moved. Her eyes opened a tiny bit. "Sei. Can you hear me?" Her eyes were half open, and her mouth moved but nothing audible came out.

"You put something in her tea?" Akil asked, looking back at Yanick.

He remained quiet but Akil continued pressing for an answer. "Yanick, answer me!"

"I put zolpidem in her tea. She will sleep for a few hours, that's all."

"Why? She is all I have to protect myself. Don't you understand that?" Akil brushed her hair from her eyes. "Sei, everything will be okay."

She mumbled as she tried to sit up.

"Here, I'll help you." He carried her over to the couch

so she could lie down. "You need rest, " he said, lowering her to the cushions. "You'll feel better in a few hours." He lifted her head gently and placed a throw pillow under her cheek.

Sei tried to speak again, but her words were more slurred than coherent.

"It's the drug, Sei. It's making you sleepy."

Her eyes remained closed but her forehead crinkled.

"No, it wasn't me, if that's what you're thinking. I'm not that stupid, but someone else is."

Akil looked over at Yanick who stood against the counter with his arms folded across his chest and a smile forming on his face. He didn't seem worried about what he had done.

"What are you up to, Yanick? You plan on dumping her someplace? She'll come for you."

"She cannot protect you forever, Akil. What will she do, stand by your side for all eternity? No, wait. She will kill the entire gang, and that will be the end of it. What about this other man you mentioned? You are in bigger trouble than you realize. This woman is not your savior."

Yanick unfolded his arms, revealing the butcher knife he held. "I'm sorry, my friend, but you are worth a lot of money."

Akil couldn't believe what his eyes and ears were relaying. He never thought Yanick would turn on him. He believed it would be safe to come to him. Yanick wasn't the type to take matters into his own hands. He was too timid of a man; one who, until now at least, seemed completely comfortable with being a follower.

"I don't understand. You would turn on your own countryman?"

Yanick laughed. He shifted his weight from one foot to the other. "Countryman? You have high aspirations," he said, pointing the knife at Akil. "You think because we are from the same country, share the same religion and beliefs, that we are beholden to each other?" He sneered. "This is about money. Survival. You used me in your trafficking scheme. You made a lot of money. I made a pittance."

"Money? You do well, Yanick. Your shop makes good money. You are not living in the streets and begging for food."

"No, I am not, but I'm also not living as comfortably as I could be," he said, waving the knife around. "You think I like living alone in the home of some other family? You think I'm content, that I don't wish for more?"

"This isn't you. The Yanick I know is hardworking, loyal. He doesn't turn on others."

Yanick shook his head. "Your sweet talk is just that. I don't believe anything you say. You don't care about me. You care only about yourself."

"That isn't true. I treat you with respect, and I've helped you in the past. I've been good to you. It's you who's doing wrong now."

Yanick drew a deep breath, and his frown intensified. "Akil, you sell young girls for sex! You are no angel."

Akil stood up. "You want to blame someone? Blame their parents for selling them," he said, pointing out the window. "I didn't kidnap them."

"If a tiger offers you to scratch his belly and then bites you, do you blame the tiger?"

"You helped!" Akil shouted back. "You drove the girls to the border. Don't act like you are innocent."

"I don't have sex with them. They're only children. You think this is something Allah approves of?" Yanick turned his head and spat. "We're not friends. I would never allow you to come in contact with my family. And if I had a daughter, I would keep her far from you. You'll get what you deserve, *inshAllah*, god-willing."

Akil let out a disgusted breath. "If I am evil, so are you. You cannot separate what I do and what you do. You're a part of it."

"What you do with those girls is one thousand times worse than anything I did or am about to do." With his other hand, Yanick removed his cell phone from his front pants pocket and dialed a number.

Chapter 44

Mdivani waited patiently in his seat for Sei and Akil to show up. At the thirty-minute mark, he still felt confident of his decision. At one hour, worry lines creased his forehead. At an hour and a half, he was sure he had either missed them or had gotten it wrong. Having to report back to Ivanovich that he had lost them wasn't appealing.

However, there was a sliver of hope.

The gang members were still waiting at the terminal. One of them, most likely their leader since he constantly berated the others in between calls on his cell phone, appeared extremely agitated. Were they also in the same boat and had no idea if Akil would come to the terminal? Mdivani shook off the thought. This was their turf. If anything, they would have eyes and ears everywhere. They were his best bet at locating Akil.

Phnom Penh had a population of one and a half million people. Sei and Akil could easily remain hidden from him, but not from the gang. No sooner had that thought crossed his mind than the restless man received a call on his cell phone and his demeanor changed. Mdivani watched him closely as he spoke on the phone. Fifteen seconds later, he ended the call and rallied the others to follow him. *Looks like they've found Akil.*

Mdivani took extra care to stay well behind the gang members as they made their way out of the station. They continued along the sidewalk. It wasn't terribly hard to tail them. They weren't expecting to be followed, and even if they did, they would never spot him. Also, the fact that they didn't bother for transport meant one thing. *Akil must be close by.*

But what Mdivani thought would only be a couple of blocks dragged into much more. Akil's location was farther than he had thought. Was someone holding him captive? Had he been injured and unable to move? Whatever the reason, time didn't appear to be of the essence.

Mdivani stuck with the gang members, figuring if they weren't worrying, neither should he. After forty minutes of navigating crowded or non-existent footpaths, the men slowed their pace. A few drew knives, others picked up whatever makeshift weapons they could find. One even snatched a broom from a shopkeeper and broke the handle off. Mdivani was surprised that none of them brandished a handgun.

The man who took the call pointed at a building and appeared to be ordering the men to spread out around it. Mdivani moved in closer with one thought on his mind: keep Akil alive.

Chapter 45

Akil stood in disbelief as he listened to Yanick relay his whereabouts to the gang. Initially he didn't think Yanick had the guts to go through with his plan, that it was nothing more than a weak threat. He believed all Yanick wanted to do was to frighten him and extort a few dollars—not actually hand him over to die. He'd even thought Yanick might be faking the phone conversation, but he heard the voice on the other end and recognized it. Akil had wildly overestimated their friendship.

"You made a big mistake," Akil said.

Yanick sneered. "I know exactly what I'm doing."

"You don't realize the trouble you have invited upon yourself. You think they will pay you a fee for turning me over? They won't pay. They don't care about people like us."

"I didn't kill that girl. I have nothing to worry about."

"But you're not one of them," Akil argued. "They only take care of their own. You're a foreigner. For all they know, you probably helped to keep me hidden."

"I'll tell them the truth."

"You don't get it, do you?" Akil shook his head as he

bit down on his lower lip. "If you go through with this, it can only end badly for both of us."

He took a step forward, and Yanick jabbed the knife. "Don't test me."

"What about Sei? What do you intend to do with her?" Akil asked, briefly glancing at her.

"Nothing. I couldn't make the call with her awake."

"I'm telling you, she will kill you."

"Then I will tell the gang they can do with her as they wish. It will make up for her killing some of their men. Akil, this is the end for you. Accept that."

Akil took another step forward, and Yanick again jabbed the knife at him. "Stay away. I'm not afraid of you."

"And I'm not afraid of you!"

Akil charged straight ahead, and as he expected, Yanick did nothing but cringe. Akil grabbed hold of the hand holding the knife, and the two wrestled for control. Both men were of similar strength resulting in a dance of pushing and pulling.

"Let go!" Akil shouted.

"No, you let go."

Akil pulled forward and spun Yanick around him, but he remained on his feet and used the momentum to swing Akil around and into one of the chairs.

Akil grunted as his thigh made contact with the wooden armrest, causing him to lose his balance. He fell into the chair, but he was still able to maintain a grip on

Yanick's hand.

Yanick jerked his arm, desperately trying to free it, but Akil was relentless in the battle. "The gang will be here any minute. Don't make it any worse than it already is, Akil."

"It's you who needs to worry."

The next time Yanick yanked his hand back, Akil used the momentum to explode out of the chair and drive a shoulder into Yanick. They fell to the floor hard, and Yanick let out a groan.

"Give up, Yanick. You can't win this fight."

Yanick said nothing, and only stared back, wide-eyed. Akil felt Yanick's grip lessen and then watched his hands fall to his side. Akil looked down to find that the knife had been driven deep into Yanick's ribcage.

"Yanick! I didn't mean to. I'm so sorry." Akil moved off of him. Only the wooden handle could be seen protruding from Yanick's torso; it rose up and down with each breath. His shirt was already soaked red.

"Everything is going to be okay." Akil used a dishcloth to stem the blood flow, causing Yanick to wince in pain.

Akil wasn't sure what to do for his friend. He couldn't call the police or an ambulance. He looked into Yanick's eyes. The fear that held them open had begun to fade. He moved his mouth.

"What is it?" Akil got down on one knee and placed his ear near Yanick's lips. "Tell me what to do."

"Help me."

Chapter 46

Yanick lay on the floor, his watery eyes begging for help, while Akil searched his pockets for the key to his car. Nothing could be done for his friend, and with the gang en route, it was simply too dangerous to remain in the flat.

"You'll be okay. I'll send for help. I promise." Akil had always excelled at giving people empty hope. It cost him nothing, rolled easily off his tongue, and made him feel better about himself.

Yanick shook his head. "Don't leave." His words were barely louder than a breath.

Akil avoided his gaze and walked over to Sei. She was still lying on the couch, unaware of the fight that had just taken place. He grabbed her by both arms and pulled her to her feet, threw her left arm around his neck, and grabbed her around the waist with his right arm. "Come on, Sei. We have to get out of here."

Her head remained flopped over to one side, and she could barely stand.

He could hear Yanick calling his name as he pulled open the front door. He refused to look back, too lazy to give Yanick yet another look of hope. A smile and the middle finger crossed his mind.

The two pushed forward through a small hallway toward an entranceway near the rear of the building—the same way Yanick had brought them to his apartment. Akil kicked the door open, and sunlight flooded the hallway. He squeezed them both through the narrow doorway and took no more than two steps before realizing he had just walked out of the furnace and into hell.

Standing in front of Akil were four members of the KK gang.

"Akil!" Ponleak shouted.

Akil instantly remembered his last phone conversation with Ponleak. *Don't worry, I'll be right there.* Empty words were all they had been.

"You have balls showing your face in Phnom Penh."

"You don't know the whole story." Akil adjusted Sei's arm around his neck. "I didn't kill Chivy. She was alive when I dropped her off."

"Why run if you are innocent?"

"You never would have believed me. You made up your mind the minute you found out she was missing."

"I'm tired of your little lies. Everyone here knows what kind of man you are: a filthy, smelly degenerate."

"You're a hypocrite. Your gang sells girls to the highest bidder. How many have you sold into slavery so they could please men worse than me? How many were the same age as Chivy or younger?"

"You could have satisfied your sick ways with another girl. You didn't have to hurt Chivy."

Akil could see that Ponleak wasn't buying his argument or his pleading look. He looked for options to run, but there was no way past Ponleak and his men. They blocked the exit from the small, fenced-in lot. It also didn't help that he still had Sei hanging off of him.

"Your friend. Did you take advantage of her too?"

"You know who she is? She's a professional. She killed many of your men. I saw it with my own eyes. How about I give her to you and we call it even? She's your type: petite and pretty. She's feisty, but those girls tend to be good fucks."

"You think I need your permission to take her?" Ponleak asked while laughing. "You can't buy or talk your way out of this, Akil. It's time for you to suffer."

Ponleak lifted his shirt to reveal a leather sheath fitted over his shoulder and across his chest. From it, he withdrew a mini-saber, the blade nearly ten inches in length. "You have nowhere to run, Akil. No friends to help you. I'm going to enjoy carving you into pieces."

Ponleak motioned for his men to close the circle around Akil. One brandished a metal pipe, another a wooden broomstick handle, and the third a large dagger.

Akil's eyes shifted back and forth as he desperately sought an escape path. Salty streams poured down his face and neck. The collar and armpits of his shirt grew damp with desperation. When the first man moved in to attack, Akil did what came naturally to him. He swung Sei around and used her as a shield.

Chapter 47

Mdivani rounded the rear corner of the building and slid to a stop in the gravel, nearly losing his balance, as he took in the scene. Akil had a very dead-looking Sei propped up in his arms, and the gang members had them surrounded.

All four men looked in Mdivani's direction. The closest one, just a few feet away, waved his knife at him. "Go now before you get hurt," he said in a thick accent.

Mdivani only smiled as a reply before stepping forward, grabbing the man's wrist and forcing it down. He followed through with a straight punch to his face, stunning him. He then bent his wrist back, wrestled control of the knife and threw it at the gang member wielding a wooden stick. The knife came to a stop in his chest.

Capitalizing on the confusion of the man he held, Mdivani yanked him forward by his wrist, gripped his arm near the elbow, and slammed it down across his thigh, snapping the bone. The man stared at the unnatural angle of his arm before letting out a blood-curdling cry. Mdivani didn't let up; he delivered a head butt, knocking the man unconscious.

He then quickly moved to the gang member with the

knife stuck in his chest. "I'll take that back, thank you," he said as he twisted it out.

With one of their own lying motionless and another bleeding to death, Ponleak and his other man closed in. Mdivani, jumped back and out of the way just as Ponleak swung his blade in a downward motion. He continued slashing to the right and then to left. Mdivani avoided each one of the strikes with ease.

"You're supposed to hit me with it. That's how a fight works," he said, flashing a smile.

Mdivani had already assessed their skills. They were amateurs. His ability far outweighed theirs, and he didn't even consider hand-to-hand combat to be one of his strengths. In fact, he saw an opportunity to do what he loved doing most: toy with his opponents. He dropped the knife he held and called the man forward.

Ponleak swung with all his strength, backing Mdivani away.

Keeping both hands behind his back, Mdivani moved his body from side to side, avoiding each attempted strike. "Missed me," he repeated after each swing. This dance continued until Mdivani felt his left heel hit the side of the building.

"Look where your cheap talk has gotten you," Ponleak said, "No place to go now."

"You sound out of breath. Do you need a minute in your corner? Maybe some water for you parched throat? I can wait here, like we've put the video game on pause."

Ponleak grunted as he swung the blade horizontally in a wide arc. Mdivani stood still, eyes wide and mocking, until the last possible moment when he dropped to crouching position. The tip of metal blade clanked against the brick building, sending a spray of red debris into the air.

Mdivani leaned over and kicked upward into Ponleak's gut, causing his opponents eyes to clench shut and a blast of air to explode from his mouth. He then executed a shoulder roll to the side and rose to his feet. Ponleak remained bent at the abdomen, his saber hanging useless by his side.

The remaining gang member raised his metal pipe like a bat and circled around Mdivani, who brought his hands to his mouth and mimed chewing his nails in fear. This didn't distract the man as he planted his left foot and swung the twenty-four inches of steel at a downward angle.

Mdivani stepped to the outside of the swing, narrowly avoiding it. The man's entire right side of his body was open to attack as his momentum continued with the pipe. But Mdivani didn't strike. Instead, he continued his lateral move until he stepped behind the man, who was just recovering from his swing.

The gang member turned to face Mdivani. But Mdivani turned in sync, keeping himself behind the man. With each turn, Mdivani duplicated the move. Left, then right, and left again.

"Argh," the man yelled in frustration.

No matter which way he spun, he could not face Mdivani. He was too fast.

By then, Ponleak had recovered and shouted for the other man to move out of the way as he advanced. "I got this punk!"

Mdivani ducked and leapt to the side, avoiding Ponleak's strike. "You got air." He quickly kicked the man with the pipe square in the chest, sending him flying backward to the ground.

By then Ponleak had wound up for another swing, and Mdivani realized his mistake. With all the fun he was having, he had failed to keep his eye on the ball that mattered the most.

Akil and Sei had disappeared.

Chapter 48

Mdivani knew that with each passing second, Akil and Sei were distancing themselves from him. He quickly disarmed Ponleak, delivered an elbow to his face, and followed with a knife slash to his chest. Ponleak decided then that he'd rather escape with a nasty chest wound than lose his life, and promptly ran.

Mdivani hurried to the front of the building, and surprisingly, the other two members of the gang were still waiting outside the entrance, unaware of what had happened. That also told him Akil and Sei hadn't passed by. He looped back and through another short passageway that opened into small parking area big enough for maybe three or four cars.

From there he spotted fresh tire tracks in the gravel of a long driveway that led to another street. He followed it and found that the traffic was at a standstill because of a red light. Feeling hopeful, Mdivani walked along the footpath and scanned the cars, but the light turned green shortly after and the spacing between the cars grew. *Where are you?*

Hope began to fade until his eyes settled on white compact vehicle waiting to make a left turn at the intersection. As the car turned, he recognized Akil in the driver's seat. *I see you.* They were too far away for Mdivani to catch up by foot. He needed a vehicle. He hurried back to the parking lot, intent on stealing a car, but his return had him facing something he wasn't expecting.

Near the other entrance into the car park were a couple of men from local law enforcement talking to a shopkeeper. *Looks like they found the bodies.* Immediately the shopkeeper pointed at Mdivani. *And now they've found me.*

One of the officers placed a call on his cell phone as they both approached Mdivani with no hint of Cambodian friendliness. Each had a hand resting on the butt of his gun; one officer was a left-hander, and the other a right-hander. Mdivani thought briefly about turning and running, but he knew if he did, he would lose any chance of catching up with Akil and Sei.

Mdivani raised his hands slowly, still unsure of what his plan was, but he knew he couldn't allow them to apprehend him. One of the officers pointed and shouted at him in Cambodian. It wouldn't be long before backup appeared, and it didn't help matters that a small crowd of nosy locals was already forming.

Mdivani bowed in an effort to help diffuse the situation, but really what he needed was a distraction, something that would give the two officers reason to drop their guard, if only for a few seconds. He still had his handgun tucked in his waistband, but he wanted to avoid leaving more bodies, especially those belonging to the local police force.

He glanced back. The driveway was empty, but turning to run left little room for him to dodge a bullet to the back. Mdivani racked his brain for something to draw their attention—the cars, the buildings, the crowd gathering…how could he utilize them?

The police were now a mere fifteen feet away, close enough they could shoot him with their eyes closed. He had allowed them to enter the dead perimeter—an area where a gunshot would be fatal. Being farther out would have given him a chance of sustaining a non-lethal wound, something survivable.

The wheels in his head continued to spin, but the only idea that seemed plausible was utilizing the one weapon he had hoped to avoid. But the longer he stood there, the farther away Akil and Sei would be. Losing their trail when he had just found it again was not an option.

The two officers watched Mdivani touch his wrists together and bow his head. They relaxed their stiff postures a bit. It appeared to them, and to the crowd, that they were seconds away from apprehending him without resistance. Shouts of admiration arose from the crowd. A few clapped their hands. One whistled his approval.

The encouragement from the crowd fueled the officers' confidence. They glanced at each other, slapped a hand on each other's back. One even turned to the crowd and waved.

It was likely their thoughts were more focused on the impending praise and likely promotions than the task at hand.

The lead officer hoisted his utility belt as he ordered the other officer to handcuff Mdivani. A cheeky smile appeared on his face as he removed his cell phone, intent on documenting the arrest. He pointed the phone at Mdivani's wrists and motioned for the other officer to proceed. However, by doing so, the officers played right into Mdivani's hands and created the one distraction he couldn't orchestrate on his own.

Chapter 49

The engine choked as Akil struggled to shift into second gear. After a few forced attempts, the gear slipped into place. He released the clutch while pressing his foot against the gas pedal, and the jerking movements of the vehicle eventually smoothed out.

Sei leaned against the passenger door of the front seat, mumbling nonsense, her eyes opening and shutting periodically. Akil wasn't sure if she was aware of what had just happened—or if bringing her along with him was such a smart move.

"Sei, we're driving out of the city."

She flopped her head in the direction of Akil's voice and said something unintelligible.

"Never mind. You make no sense." Only time, sleep, and plenty of fluids would help.

When he felt they were far enough away from the assassin and the gang to be safe for a moment, he pulled the vehicle over and dug inside Sei's pockets for a few euros to purchase bottled water from a street vendor. Akil opened one bottle and held it to Sei's mouth. "You must drink. It'll help."

She continued to question why she felt so sleepy.

"Yanick drugged you. I'll explain later." He grabbed her hand and placed the bottle in it. "Just keep on drinking the water."

Akil put the car in gear and merged back into traffic. The afternoon rush hour was in full swing. He slammed a hand against the steering wheel and cursed their situation briefly before his thoughts turned back to what had happened at Yanick's place.

At first, he assumed things had gone from crap to worse, but then the assassin attacked the gang. Akil had been just as confused as the gang had been, but he wasn't about to stick around to find out why. He carried Sei away the first chance he had.

None of it made any sense, but Akil accepted it as good fortune. He could still hear them fighting when he'd sat Sei in the front seat of Yanick's vehicle; he didn't dare hesitate for fear he would end up in the same position he'd just escaped.

Akil looked over at Sei, hoping the water would bring her back to life; her slow recovery worried him a bit. He drummed the top of the steering wheel with his thumbs as his eyes peered into the rearview mirror. Every step on the brake was an opportunity to be caught. Sure, Yanick was the reason for the gang showing up, but what about the assassin? He was able to locate them a third time. Did he have an array of resources at his fingertips? A drone? A satellite? Or was it something as simple as following the gang?

After twenty minutes or so, the spacing between cars widened, and Akil was able to drive forward in a gear other than first and second. He used his shoulder to wipe his nose and relaxed a bit.

They continued driving southwest toward the edge of the city on Highway 4, which would take them to the town of Koh Kong, and the Thai border. It wasn't heavily traveled because the highway was notoriously known to be the most dangerous one in all of Cambodia due the severity of traffic accidents along its route. Most people took the well-maintained Highway 5 or 6 toward the Poipet border crossing. Akil figured if the gang or the assassin had guessed where he was heading, they would cover Poipet.

Besides being chased, Akil was worried about Sei's condition. He thought the effects of the drug would have lessened, but she seemed just as woozy then as she had in Yanick's apartment. He figured her diminutive size was the reason. He also started to wonder again if he really needed her.

The border wasn't too far away, and as far as he could ascertain, no one seemed to be following them. *Why not get rid of her?* They would have separated eventually. What would be the harm in parting sooner rather than later? It was farmland in all directions from there on out. It would only take seconds to dump her body in one of the many irrigation ditches on the side of the highway. *Ah, to be free once again, chasing the little ones.*

Chapter 50

The officer swung the cuff down toward Mdivani's left wrist. But Mdivani was faster. He grabbed the officer's left forearm and replaced his own wrist with that of the officer. *Click*, the hardened metal cuff locked itself into place. Mdivani then grabbed the arm of the officer holding the cell phone and slapped the other cuff around his wrist.

The left hand of one officer was handcuffed to right hand of the other officer resulting in a tug of war as to who would draw his weapon first and how—each man's holster sat on the opposite hip of his free hand.

As they continued their struggle, Mdivani slammed both of their heads together. *Thunk!* One officer lost consciousness and immediately dropped to the gravel, pulling the other officer to his knees. Dazed, he desperately tried to get back to his feet, but Mdivani planted his left foot and swung his right leg around. The hardened tip of his shoe slammed into the officer's left temple, sending him straight to the ground, his body convulsing in fits.

A few seconds later the officer's movements slowed, but by then Mdivani had already exited the parking area. He wasn't sure if the kick had killed the officer and didn't care.

His only concern at the moment was whether he could pick up Akil and Sei's trail.

While on the run, Mdivani pulled up Google Maps on his phone and evaluated his next move based on the direction Akil and Sei had taken. That road eventually turned into Highway 4, which ended at the Koh Kong border crossing into Thailand.

He got into the first taxi he saw and asked the driver to take him to Koh Kong, but the driver declined with a friendly smile. Mdivani withdrew his handgun, leaned forward, and pressed the barrel against the man's temple. "Drive!"

As the taxi approached the outskirts of the city, Mdivani had yet to see Akil and Sei anywhere. Part of him hoped that he would, but he knew they had gained a fairly large head start. The thought did cross his mind that he might be wrong about where they were heading, but so far he'd been right more than he'd been wrong. He had to trust his gut.

For them to come to Phnom Penh, where the threat of those gang members existed, there had to be a good reason. They needed something. And whatever it was, it wasn't of value to Sei. If it were, they would have parted, but again they stuck together. She still needs him. That was the premise Mdivani was working on as Phnom Penh faded behind him.

After thirty minutes of driving outside of Phnom Penh,

the driver's whimpering had exhausted Mdivani's patience. He ordered the man to pull to the side of the road. When the car behind them passed and was a safe distance away, he had the driver exit the car and then executed him with a single bullet to the back of the head. The body tumbled into the ditch that ran along the side of the road. Mdivani moved into the driver's seat, buckled up, and pulled back onto the road.

Chapter 51

I drew a sharp breath as my eyes shot open. *Where am I?* My eyelids fluttered as I struggled to focus in the dark. I swallowed, but my tongue stuck and my throat followed suit. I was still dressed; I could feel my clothing, even my shoes. *Calm down, Sei.* My hands were clenching something soft beneath me. *A blanket?* I relaxed my grip and rubbed the sleep from my eyes, wondering how long I had been unconscious and a little surprised that I wasn't dead.

I closed my eyes and inhaled deeply for a few moments before propping myself up on my elbows. My chest felt heavy and my head dizzy with a slight throbbing. I glanced around, and my surroundings slowly came into to focus. There was a small desk pushed up against a wall with a chair in front of it. The short boxy thing next to it looked like a dresser. I could see a window with curtains drawn across it. At least it looked like a window. A soft hum and the cool air told me there was an air conditioner somewhere. My blouse was sticking to my back, and I reached behind me to pull it away from my skin. The material was slightly damp. There were two doors, one ajar but it was too dark to see inside. *Bathroom?* It was clear to me that I was in a bedroom and very much alone.

Did he run again?

I swung my legs over the side of the bed. On the floor there was a liter of bottled water, and seeing it triggered an itch in my throat. As I gulped the water, I had remembered Akil mentioning something about Yanick drugging me but the reasons were unclear. I wasn't in pain, and all my senses appeared to be intact. The effects of the drug seemed to have mostly worn off.

A quick pat down of my pants pockets told me I still had my money and cell phone. I squinted at my watch; it was a little after eight thirty p.m. If Akil had abandoned me, why not take my money or my phone? I stood and walked over to the desk; the balls of my feet ached for the first couple of steps. There wasn't a note or any indication elsewhere in the room that he would be returning.

I moved the curtain to the side and looked out the window. There wasn't a view, just the gray bare wall of another building about ten feet away. The alley was dark with the exception of the entrance where a street lamp was positioned. I pressed my face against the window and peered in the other direction—a dark dead end.

A copy of the *Phnom Penh Post* lay folded on the desk. I switched on the small desk lamp for a better look. It was printed in English and dated two days earlier. An educated guess told me I was still in Cambodia, but I questioned whether it was Phnom Penh.

I took a quick peek outside the door and saw a short, bare hall. There were two other closed doors but they had no markings indicating whether they were bedrooms like mine. I could only surmise that I was in a small guesthouse or place where rooms were rented by the hour. I closed the door and sat on the edge of the bed. I could feel the heat rise in my cheeks as the realization that Akil had left me set in. *I told him not to run.*

In that moment, everything I had gone through filled my thoughts: fending off multiple attacks and bribing officials, not to mention just having to be around that despicable person. To think after all of that, he had the upper hand. I had to wonder if this was his intention from the very start.

If truth were told, I was angrier with myself than I was with him. I had allowed this to happen. From the moment I discovered the truth about my daughter, my emotions had clouded my judgment. It seemed as if I could rationalize every decision as necessary. Desperation drove me. I felt powerless. I wanted so badly to find my daughter that I essentially saw hope where there was very little. How else could I explain the situation I was now in? I swore to myself then that if I ever crossed paths with Akil, I would show no mercy. I had just begun to contemplate my options when I heard the deadbolt on the door slide open.

Chapter 52

"You're up," Akil said, appearing in the doorway. He felt the wall for the light switch.

"Don't. Leave it off."

"Okay." He closed the door behind him.

I had gotten myself so worked up that when I saw Akil, I wanted nothing more than to charge at him and snap his neck. "I told you to never run from me."

"I didn't. I got us food," he said, holding up two plastic bags. "You were still sleeping."

I didn't care that he was telling the truth. It was only a few seconds ago I thought everything was for naught, that a conversation with the nurse who held my daughter would not happen. I had given Akil too much power and allowed him to determine the terms of our agreement. No more.

"Where are we?"

Akil placed the bags on the desk. "We're in a small town near Talat. I'm not sure of the name."

"Why did we stop?"

"I was worried about your condition." He took a seat on the chair and explained everything to me from the moment Yanick drugged me until we reached the guesthouse.

"You've endangered my life one too many times, Akil. It stops now."

He opened his mouth to speak but instead shook his head, turning away while waving off my last remark.

"You think this is a game? You think you can treat me like you do those girls—like something disposable?"

"No, I don't—"

"Stop lying!"

"It's me they're trying to kill. Don't forget that," he shot back.

I exploded off the bed, and my right hand latched on to his skinny neck. The momentum tipped the chair back, and I rode him down, his head hitting the floor hard. I slid up and straddled his chest and gripped his neck with both hands. He tried to bat them away, but I increased the pressure, my thumb digging into the soft flesh just to the side of his vocal cord. "I don't care what happens to you. I care about what happens to me."

He was unable to speak. His eyes grew wide. Saliva spilled from the side of his mouth. At that moment, I didn't care if I killed him. I wanted him to pay for his involvement with my daughter's kidnapping, for what he did to Yesmine's daughter and all the other little girls who had crossed his path. But I couldn't. Not just yet.

I released my grip and got off of him. He gasped for air and rubbed his throat as he leered at me from the floor, his chest heaving up and down.

I took a seat on the bed and a moment to calm down before speaking to him again. "Are you positive the assassin attacked the gang members and it wasn't the other way around?" I asked.

Akil nodded and sat up, still rubbing his neck. "That's how it looked to me."

"And when we left, they were still fighting?"

"He had already killed two of them."

Why would the assassin attack the gang? That made absolutely no sense to me unless the conditions of his contract stated he needed to be the one to eliminate Akil and not the gang. Still I couldn't see why the Wolf would care as to who killed Akil or how.

"You said this assassin was hired to kill me. How much is he being paid?" Akil asked.

I thought it strange to inquire. "Twenty thousand euros, from what I understand. I can't be sure, though."

"Twenty thousand? They must *really* want me dead."

"They do, and it's time you told me the name of the nurse."

"But we're not at the border. That was the deal."

"You're safe enough. The deal is complete. Tell me her name and where I can find her."

"The border isn't far—only a three-hour drive. We can cross in the morning."

"This isn't a negotiation." I said as I stood up.

So did Akil.

"I'm not afraid of you. You can't keep threatening me," he said with a raised voice.

I closed the distance between us, hooked my right arm under his neck, and swung my body completely around, landing on his back. I applied a chokehold. Akil gagged for air.

"You need to understand that I am in charge." I applied more pressure, and he dropped to his knees.

He grabbed at my forearms in an effort to pull them away, all while trying to shake me off. This of course was wasted effort. My legs were hooked around his skinny waist and locked in. I applied the pressure to his throat in bursts, enough for him to take a tiny breath before I clamped down again. It wouldn't render him unconscious, just mimic the feeling of choking.

After a few seconds of this, he tapped rapidly on my arm. I released the pressure and jumped off his back. He fell to all fours, coughing and breathing deeply at once.

"Her name and where I can find her," I repeated.

Akil said nothing.

"I will not ask a third time."

Between coughs, he told me her name. "Amina Jelassi. She works at a hospital." He turned over and leaned back on his arms. "But I don't know the name of the hospital. I swear."

"Not knowing which hospital she works at isn't very

helpful." I picked up the chair; the four legs were wobbly. "It's the difference of whether this information has merit or is worthless." I slammed the chair down on the floor. Two of the legs broke off, one of them splintering into a sharp point. "Akil, you should know that I didn't partake in this journey because I'm fond of you." I picked up the makeshift stake. "It's not because I pity your situation or care about your safety." I walked over to Akil. "And if I'm to be truthful here, it hasn't much to do with your role in the abduction of my child, seeing that it was minimal at best."

He began to scoot away from me. "So you believe me?"

"But there is good reason for your life to end."

"Wait! You said you wouldn't hurt me. You made a promise."

I stood over him. "And I always keep them."

His eyes locked on the stake in my hand. "I made a promise to Yesmine. I told her when I found you I would deal with you." I raised the stake high above my head. "You're being dealt with."

Chapter 53

Mdivani kept his eyes peeled as he drove through the small towns along Highway 4. He couldn't think of any reason for Akil and Sei to turn off the main road. At most, he figured they would stop for a bathroom break or to pick up food.

Catch-up came in a small village. Mdivani had to double back for a second look at the white vehicle parked in front of a restaurant. It had been a while since he saw it, and when he had, it was from a distance. Upon closer inspection, he saw it was a Suzuki Swift, maybe three or four years old. He was seventy-percent sure he had located the right vehicle. He peered into the restaurant and scanned the surrounding shops but saw no sign of them. *Did they ditch the car? Are they still here?* Mdivani glanced at his watch; it was fifteen after nine at night. He had a decision to make: camp out or continue searching.

He drove thirty yards farther down the road and parked. He bought a newspaper, took a seat at a table outside a nearby coffee shop, and kept an eye on the car. *I'll give it fifteen minutes.*

And he did, but still he didn't see the two. Mdivani

walked back toward the vehicle, wondering if they had indeed abandoned it and stolen another or if they were possibly spending the night here. The border wasn't that far. Why stop?

He turned to the small restaurant, basically a large open space filled with ten metal tables accompanied by plastic stools. Two tables were occupied by patrons. There was no front wall or window enclosing the restaurant; it was wide open. The open kitchen was located at the rear, essentially a couple of men operating two searing woks and a prep counter where two women put the dishes together. Whatever they were cooking triggered his stomach to growl, but eating wasn't an option at the moment.

He approached a server sweeping the sidewalk. "Excuse me. English?"

The boy—a teenager—nodded. "Little." He squeezed his forefinger and thumb together.

Mdivani removed his phone and showed him a picture of Akil. "You see this man? He drives the white car," he said, pointing.

The teen leaned in for a better look and crinkled his pierced brow before nodding yes. Mdivani showed him Sei's picture, and he received the same response. "Did they eat here?"

"No," the teen said.

"Where did they go? Which way?" Mdivani pointed up and down the street.

The teen pointed, but it wasn't left or right. "Upstairs. We have guestroom."

Chapter 54

Mdivani couldn't believe what he had heard and inquired again.

"Yes, I sure," the teen said. "They come maybe two hour ago. You want room?"

"No, I want to find my friends. We separated back in Phnom Penh."

The teen frowned.

"I got lost."

"Oh, okay. You want go to room?"

"Are they there now?"

"I think so. Man come for food. He take away but I not see lady. Him also tell me not bother them."

Mdivani chewed his lower lip as he weighed his options—*wait until they vacate the room or confront them now?* "Do you have an extra room?"

The teen nodded. "Fifteen dollar."

Mdivani agreed to the price, and the boy took him upstairs to the second floor. "Your friends in this room."

Mdivani grabbed hold of the teen's arm just before he was about to knock on the door. "I want to surprise my friends, okay?"

The teen shrugged and led Mdivani to the room next door.

"Okay, thank you," Mdivani said "What time does the restaurant close?"

"Ten thirty," the teen replied.

Mdivani closed the door and pressed his ear against it, listening until he heard the teen's rubber flip-flips clomping down the stairs. He hurried over to the wall he shared with Akil and Sei's room and pressed his ear against it. He heard nothing but the distant sound of running water. He couldn't readily determine if it was coming from inside their room, perhaps a sink or a shower, or if it were simply the pipes in the wall. He moved over to the window, opened it, and looked outside. The alley was dark; there didn't appear to be any lights on in their room. *Maybe they're sleeping.*

Mdivani closed the window. He removed his gun and checked his ammo count—four bullets left with one in the chamber. He switched out the mag with a fully loaded one from his knapsack. He then screwed the sound suppressor onto the Beretta.

Once again, he pressed his ear against the wall—still just the sound of running water. Mdivani couldn't wait any longer. He had to make a move and know for sure if they were there or if this was all a ruse, an attempt to cover their tracks.

He peeked out into the empty hall. The clanking of the metal spatulas against the woks traveled up the stairs, but he heard no footsteps. He held his weapon close to his body at chest height and stepped quietly over to Akil and Sei's room. Thoughts that he might have fallen for their simple trick began to populate in his head. He could feel the beats of his heart increase, fueling the boil of his blood and the throbbing in his neck.

He stepped back and fired twice at the deadbolt lock before kicking the door open and bursting into the room, weapon out in front.

He swiveled left, right, and left again before heading toward the bathroom door. He checked the knob; it was unlocked. Mdivani took a step back and kicked his boot against the door, sending it flying inward.

He stood still with his feet apart, knees bent, arms out front, peering down the barrel of his gun. Sitting on the toilet was Akil. The aiming sights of Mdivani's gun were positioned in the center of his chest, only Akil didn't move—not even a flinch. As his eyes adjusted to the dim light, Mdivani understood why. A large wooden stake protruding from Akil's chest had finished the job for him.

Chapter 55

Sei!

Mdivani placed two fingers on Akil's neck, then
moved his head from side to side. *Warm. Pliable. She killed
him recently.* He flipped on the light switch and saw a pile
of blood-stained towels in the corner of the bathroom.
Akil's shirt soaked up much of the fluid that leaked out of
him before it coagulated. He turned the light off and stepped
out of the bathroom.

Even with the lights off, he could see there wasn't any
blood on the bed. He removed a pen light from his
knapsack, bent down, and scanned the floor. He found a
thin red streak. *She killed him here, moved him into the
bathroom and then cleaned. She wanted a head start.*

Mdivani figured Sei must have retrieved the
information she needed from him. Either that, or she got
tired of babysitting, which was a real possibility, but he had
his money on the first scenario. It was logical, since both of
them were alive not too long ago. If Sei no longer thought
Akil was an asset, then neither did Mdivani. There wouldn't
be any reason to keep Akil alive, and he wasn't in breach of
the Wolf's directive. He whipped out his phone and snapped

a photo of Akil on the toilet. *The Wolf will like this.*

Mdivani tucked his weapon back into the waistband of his jeans. He then closed the bathroom door and exited the room. Downstairs he ran into the same teen boy, who was busy refilling the condiment containers on a table.

"You come to eat? We close soon," he said.

There were two diners still eating but aside from them, the restaurant was empty. The kitchen crew had already begun to clean their workspace.

"No, I'm fine. I ate with my friends." Mdivani said as he mimicked forking food into his mouth. He then removed his wallet from his back pocket. "I'll pay for one more night. Me and my friends."

The boy took the money.

"You keep the change." Mdivani smiled.

"Thank you," the boy mumbled before returning to his duties.

Mdivani exited the restaurant and headed to the taxi he stole earlier. Most of the residents of the village seemed to be in bed. A couple of motorbikes zoomed by, but foot traffic was non-existent. He saw only a few lit windows in the nearby apartment buildings, and apart from the twenty-four-hour convenience store farther down the road, all of the shops were closed.

He continued driving west on Highway 4. He wasn't necessarily worried about picking up Sei's trail. He knew enough to conclude that someone who was at the clinic that day was located in Thailand, most likely Bangkok. What he wasn't sure of was whether Sei knew exactly where this person was. Mdivani pressed the pedal harder, and the taxi picked up speed. *Okay, Sei. Let's see who reaches the golden prize first.*

Chapter 56

"Amina!" The shrill voice penetrated the thin door. "When will dinner be ready?"

Amina sat quietly on the toilet, trying to savior the few minutes of peace she could have while at home, but the voice rang out again, pecking at her to answer. She let out a soft breath, finished her business, and flushed.

She exited the tiny bathroom/shower space into a room that wasn't really that much bigger. The small apartment was composed of a single room with two beds pushed up against the wall, a flat-screen television on a stand, a short dresser with a mirror attached, and a standing closet next to it. A bevy of small plastic storage containers holding clothes, food, and other necessities were spread out over the floor.

There wasn't much space to maneuver in the room; it seemed like something or someone occupied every inch of floor. The room was no bigger than thirty-five square meters, and six people lived there: three adults and three small children. It was impossible for two people to walk in the room at the same time without turning their bodies sideways and brushing against each other.

A woman sat on the bed with her back up against the wall, her snug shirt tucked into the multiple rolls along her stomach. Her name was Houda, a distant relative from Amina's father's side.

"Amina, everybody is hungry. What is taking so long?" she asked, letting out a disappointed breath as she cycled through the channels on the TV with the remote. Sitting on either side of her were two little girls, twins. Their names were Nada and Amira, and they were five years old. Nada stuck her tongue out at Amina.

"I'm sorry," Amina said, keeping her head down. "I still have to chop the vegetables."

She stepped over the other child, Josef, who was three. He lay on the floor making growling noises as he played with two plastic toy dinosaurs. Sleeping on the other bed was Houda's husband, Dadi. Sleeping seemed to be all he ever did. He never had reliable work, and when he did, he always managed to get himself fired. Houda ran a small coffee stand outside their building in the morning, but aside from that, she kept her behind attached to the bed as well.

Amina was the only one in the household who had a full-time job. She worked twelve-hour shifts, six days a week as a nurse. On top of that, she was also responsible for doing all the cooking, cleaning, and shopping, and on her day off, there was always something that Houda needed her to do. In return for her all of her contributions, Amina was allowed to sleep on a thin mattress on the floor.

That night she had to work an extra hour at the hospital and didn't arrive home until seven p.m. Instead of getting dinner started, Houda sat in her usual spot and waited for Amina, only to complain non-stop from the moment she set foot in the room.

"We are doing you a favor by letting you stay here. You should appreciate our kindness," she barked.

"I do," Amina replied softly.

She noticed that Houda hadn't bothered to bathe the kids yet. So amid preparing dinner, Amina had to ensure that each child was bathed. By the time she finished her duties, it was always nearing eleven p.m. The three kids were usually fast asleep on one bed, and Houda and Dadi were snoring on the other. Amina would take that opportunity to escape to the rooftop of the five-story apartment building located in the On Nut district of Bangkok.

It was only on the rooftop that she felt she could relax and enjoy what little time she had to herself before going to bed. Her shift at the hospital started at six a.m., which required waking up at four thirty.

Amina took a seat in her favorite place, a molded plastic chair between two elevated steel water reservoirs. It was far enough from the hum of the air vents to be quiet, and she was hidden from sight, which she preferred. From there she had a clear view of the night sky, unfettered by the clotheslines strung across the other half of the rooftop.

She removed a plastic bag from the waistband of her pants. Inside was a bottle of peach-flavored iced tea. The drink had warmed by then, but Amina didn't care. She had to keep it hidden from the children or they would ask to have some. Houda always demanded that Amina share whatever food or drink she brought home. That usually meant turning it over to the ungrateful little ones. It was not that Amina didn't want to share with the children; it was just that, when she first moved in, she always gave what little she had, but there was never any reciprocation. So she stopped.

Amina unscrewed the plastic cap and savored the first sip as she gazed at the stars above. The sky was exceptionally clear. The Southern Cross constellation shone bright that night, as did the mighty Leo, the Cancer crab, and the serpent Hydra. Amina loved gazing at the stars while dreaming of better days ahead. She longed for a life of her own, to be free from the demands of Houda and her family.

Moving to Thailand was the first step to escaping her troubled past. She thought immigrating to France from Tunisia would provide her with a fulfilling and comfortable life, but it had turned out to be exactly the opposite.

From living a meager existence in the crime-ridden La Cite and working grueling hours at a hospital for low pay, her life was worse in France than in Tunisia. Amina felt like a shoe stuck in the mud with no solid ground in sight. She barely made enough to keep a roof over her head, let alone able to put money aside to carve a better life. Schooling seemed out of reach, even within France's generous socialist system. Moving to another country cost money, which she lacked, plus the bevy of problems faced by illegal immigrants would only add to the weight on her shoulders. She at least had legal immigrant status in France.

So when the job offer to help deliver a baby presented itself, Amina jumped at the opportunity to make extra cash on the side. Payment was ten thousand euros—unheard of, but Amina didn't question. She didn't want to appear problematic and lose the opportunity.

Accepting that job should have given her life a much-needed lift, but it ended up burying her further. The burden of having unknowingly partaken in a kidnapping scheme was too much for her to bear—that, and the threat made to her from the man in charge to keep her mouth shut or he would make sure she never saw another day. With money in hand, Amina made the decision to create a new life, in a new country.

While things weren't grand at the tiny room in the old building on Soi 20, Amina kept dreaming and pushing herself forward. Since her first paycheck from the hospital, she had been saving a little every week in a bank account hidden from Houda. *Small steps*, she told herself. *One day, I'll be free.*

Chapter 57

By the off chance we were being followed, I decided not to take the car after exiting the room through the window. Instead, for fifty euros, I hitched a ride with a trucker passing through the village Akil and I had stopped in. I half expected trouble from him, but he kept his thoughts to himself and his hands on the steering wheel. He lived to haul another load.

Crossing the Koh Kong border was uneventful, given the time of night. The set up was similar to when we'd crossed the Vietnam/Cambodia border: stamped out of one country and stamped into the next. Not many people needed or wanted to cross at that hour. The entire process took fifteen minutes, not that I kept track. I traveled on a French passport, which afforded me visa-exempt status. As a tourist, I was allowed thirty days in the Kingdom of Thailand.

On the Thai side of the border there were a few food vendors selling noodles, skewered grilled meats, and a papaya salad called *som tum*. I grabbed two skewers and a bottle of water before negotiating a fee with one of the taxi drivers.

We arrived in Bangkok a little after nine in the
morning. The drive wasn't terrible. We made one bathroom
stop, and much like the trucker, the taxi driver paid me no
attention. It was a significant departure from my last long
drive, with Kostas; the only time he had stopped talking was
to draw a breath.

Since I had no idea where Amina lived or worked, I
studied Google Maps on my phone and determined the
Asoke Skytrain terminal was a good central location. I
checked into the Westin, only a few steps away. Once in my
room, I took a shower, ordered breakfast from room service,
and got to work.

Amina Jelassi was a nurse working and living in
Bangkok. That was the information I had to go on. I also
had Kostas run her name. I couldn't be certain if it would
lead to anything, but I didn't want to rule out that
possibility.

I logged on to the Wi-Fi service with my smartphone
and began compiling a list of all the major hospitals in
Bangkok. I left out any hospital in the outer-lying districts
and all of the small clinics—there were too many of them. I
could systematically begin to target them if my original
approach turned up empty, but I hoped it would not come to
that.

My plan forward was simple in nature. I intended to
visit each hospital and ask the staff if Amina worked there.
It would be time consuming, but it would give me a decent

shot at locating her. She was new to the city, had recently started a job, and was of Tunisian descent; surely those characteristics ticked the box for sticking out.

I didn't take long to draw up a list. There were nine hospitals in central Bangkok, and the one that made the most sense to me was an international hospital located not far from my hotel. I had already determined that I would pose as a local insurance agent who needed to speak with Amina regarding a medical procedure she had previously been involved with. I figured the average staff member wouldn't question that kind of inquiry. After I finished my list, I popped downstairs and bought a cream pantsuit and suitable shoes from the department store attached to the hotel. By the time I headed out, it was near noon.

Bumrungrad International Hospital was a ten-minute ride away by motorbike taxi. Upon my arrival, I immediately saw that the hospital was spread out over three separate buildings, with an endless supply of medical tourists, mostly from Arab and Western countries, flowing in and out of the entrances.

I headed inside the building nearest me, and the first thought that popped into my head was that I had entered the lobby of a Hyatt. There were high ceilings, leather seating, white marble flooring, art on the walls, and vases adorning every table. The only thing missing was an atrium and a decorative fountain. I understood why it was considered the premier international hospital in all of South Asia.

I searched the large directory set in granite. Obstetrics was located on the sixteenth floor. Since Amina assisted in the delivery of my baby, I assumed this was where I would find her.

The elevator chimed and the doors opened to a carpeted foyer complete with a large flower arrangement, mood lighting, and soft classical music. Straight ahead, sitting behind a reception desk, was the smiling face of nurse dressed in a white uniform with a throwback nurse's cap on her head. I didn't think those working in the medical profession wore anything but blue or gray scrubs these days.

The seating area was occupied by women in various stages of pregnancy, some with their husbands or their mothers, a few by themselves. To the rear of the seats were two counters: one to pay for services, the other to pick up prescriptions.

"English?" I asked the nurse.

"Yes, of course," she said with a pleasant smile.

"My name is Amanda Shin. I work for Siam Medical Insurance. I need to speak with a nurse by the name of Amina Jelassi. The phone we have on file appears to be disconnected, and I've had to resort to finding her through other means," I said, making a walking motion with my fingers. "Could you tell me if she's on the schedule today?"

The nurse gave me an inquisitive look at first but conceded. "Could you please repeat the name?"

"Amina Jelassi."

"It doesn't sound familiar. Are you sure she works at this hospital and in obstetrics?"

"This was the employment information she had given us."

She typed briefly on her keyboard and then scrolled while looking at her monitor. "I don't see that name in our department. Sorry. If she did work here, it wasn't for very long."

I nodded my agreement. "Yes, it appears that's the case." I rolled my eyes. "This is going to be a long day."

The nurse smiled once more and wished me luck.

I took out my list and crossed off Bumrungrad, thinking my approach may not be as laborious as I had anticipated.

Chapter 58

Mdivani arrived in Bangkok at eleven a.m., later than he had intended. He had taken a wrong turn on his way to Koh Kong and discovered his mistake only after driving for thirty minutes in the wrong direction. When he reached the border, he ditched the taxi on the Cambodian side, crossed over, and hired a Thai taxi parked next to couple of vendors selling street food.

He didn't need to research a central location because he had visited Bangkok on numerous occasions. He instructed the taxi driver to take him to the Grand Sheraton Hotel located next to the Asoke Skytrain terminal, just opposite the Westin.

Mdivani knew the Metropolitan Rapid Transit (MRT), Bangkok's underground system, also intersected with the skytrain at that point. Between those two options, taxis, and motorbikes, he had a variety of ways to move about the city.

Mdivani always traveled with three passports, and he crossed the border and checked into the hotel with a different name than the one he used in Vietnam. Before heading up to his room, he purchased a pair of slacks and a dress shirt from one of the boutiques inside the hotel. He thought about heading over to the Robinson Department Store across the street to purchase a new pair of shoes to replace his badly scuffed pair, but opted instead to have the hotel give them a shine.

Once settled into his room, he placed an order for room service and then took a hot shower. He had just finished toweling off when his food arrived: a club sandwich and fries.

Dressed in the hotel's fluffy white robe, he removed a small tablet from his knapsack and sat on the bed. The Wolf had provided him with information on all of the contracts: a photo, the job they were hired to do, and their last known address. Mdivani scanned the pictures and began mentally crossing off the people who were already dead: Feki, Delacroix, and Akil. That left six individuals: five nurses and another man hired to provide security.

Akil had been hired to provide security, so it wouldn't be unreasonable to think he had known the other guard. Perhaps they both fled France together. The others involved were nurses. Would it be beyond belief for Akil to have known one of them? The nurses were all from Paris but lived in different neighborhoods, except for one: Amina Jelassi. She lived in La Cite, the same location Akil had lived in. *Hmmm, she's a strong contender.* So Mdivani narrowed it down to the other security guard and the one nurse. *Which one of you is hiding in Bangkok?*

With the information in hand, completing the contracts

should have been a breeze, but something had spooked the workers. All but Delacroix had fled their homes and gone into hiding. Somehow they found out they had been used to orchestrate a kidnapping. The thinking in the Wolf's camp was that Delacroix had tipped them off. The workers were smart to run.

From what little Mdivani understood of what had happened that day, they were all told they would be helping with the childbirth of a VIP. Hence the secrecy and the need for armed men providing security. Still, it was hard to cover up the disappearance of a newborn.

Nurse or security? Mdivani continued to mull over the options as he bit into the overstuffed sandwich. Akil had to have known the person he was meeting fairly well to lead Sei there. It was likely that Akil and that other person traveled to the region together and then separated. Both a security guard and a nurse could find employment in Bangkok, but it would be especially easy for Amina. She had legal status in France, and all the proper paperwork and contacts to support her resume. The security guard didn't share the same status, but what requirements are really needed to be a security guard at a construction site or a parking lot?

Did that *mean* it was Amina? Not necessarily. Both could be working as illegal immigrants in Thailand. Mdivani knew it wasn't hard for immigrants to live and work in the country illegally, though if Amina wanted a job as a nurse in a proper hospital, she would require legal visa documentation and a work permit. The guard could easily find work doing odd jobs and be paid under the table. With that said, legal requirements for both could be easily purchased on the black market.

Mdivani ate a couple of fries as he contemplated the dilemma. In his head he kept coming back to the security guard. It just made the most sense. He couldn't see a person like Akil knowing a person like Amina, even if they did live in the same complex. All three were Tunisian immigrants, and La Cite was home to a large Tunisian community—it could be coincidental that they all lived in the same area, but he felt strongly that the guards would know each other. Mdivani couldn't shake the thought from his head. There was no reason to. Except, he suddenly realized there was.

Chapter 59

I know it's you.

Mdivani scooted back on the king-size bed and leaned against the backboard with his legs out straight and the tablet resting vertically on his stomach. The picture of Amina Jelassi had been enlarged to fill the entire screen. According to her file, Amina was twenty-seven years old. She had thick, chocolate-brown hair that came to her shoulders, piercing hazel eyes, and a tiny mole located near the right corner of her mouth. She was roughly five foot six, of average weight with ample bosoms—a pretty girl by anyone's standard.

It has to be you, Mdivani thought. *You have something to lose.*

The turning point had to do with their employment statuses. Amina had a real profession. She was a trained nurse, hired to assist Delacroix with the birth. The other man hired for security had nothing listed as his profession. Any street thug could be given a handgun and told to watch the door. Mdivani figured he was in a similar boat as Akil and bounced around from one odd job to the next. A loser.

But Amina had invested in her career. She had

something concrete to lose should she be caught up in a kidnapping scandal. She had real reason to distance herself. It made sense.

Bangkok was a large metropolis with Western standards. Medical tourism was burgeoning business with patients flocking to Thailand from neighboring countries as far as the US and UK. Amina would easily find employment here. She could continue her lawful life.

Mdivani took another bite of his sandwich and then a sip of the coffee he had also ordered. It was lukewarm, so he drank the entire cup in one fell swoop. He then began mentally compiling a list of hospitals. He had a name, a profession, and a picture. He couldn't be sure what information Sei held. She had a name; he assumed that much. She might even know the hospital she worked at, but Mdivani didn't want to think negatively.

He needed to move fast. Bumrungrad International Hospital topped his list. He had visited it before and knew its exact location. He could continue working on the list while on the move. He called the front desk for his shoes and then changed into the clothing he'd purchased earlier. Minutes later, he was straddling the seat of a motorbike taxi and zipping along Sukhumvit Road.

Chapter 60

Next on my list was BNH, Bangkok Nursing Home Hospital. Much like Bumrungrad, it was well established and known to treat both Thai-and English-speaking patients. I assumed Amina wasn't well versed in Thai, so she probably had to work at a hospital that serviced a decent number of English-speaking patients. At that point, I simply wanted to insert as much rational thought into how I prioritized the hospitals I went to, rather than using just location as the determining factor.

I opted for a taxi when I left Bumrungrad. While en route, I checked Google Maps on my phone to get an idea of where BNH was located in conjunction to the next one on my list: Samitivej Hospital. Bumrungrad, BNH, and Samitivej were the biggest and most popular in Bangkok.

BNH was located in the Silom district. Samitivej was located in the opposite direction, clear across town in the Thonglor neighborhood. As always, the search continued to stretch itself. As I settled in for what would be at least a twenty-five minute ride, my thoughts drifted to Mui.

Before finding out she was alive, I did think about her, but it was always in the past tense. What sort of child would she have been? Shy? Rambunctious? A little diva? Strong and independent? A warrior like her mother? That would have been the one instance where I wouldn't want her to follow in my footsteps.

There was an enormous load of guilt on my shoulders, as if I somehow should have known she wasn't dead. My motherly intuition should have kicked in. Alarms should have sounded. A nagging should have lived inside of me like an unreachable itch. She had remained curled up inside of me for nine months. Fed off of me. Kicked me. Hurt me. Shouldn't that have created the unbreakable bond?

Was it wrong that I had simply accepted her death? Was that a sign that I wasn't motherly, that I was unable to raise a child and shower it with the love it needs? Was this punishment for my profession, the universe's way of saying I didn't deserve to bring a life in this world when I had taken so many? *When I find you, Mui, I will never let go. That I promise.*

My thoughts about her in the present were different. Did she have enough to eat, proper clothes to wear, or even a comfy bed to sleep on? Was someone showing her affection, giving her a hug, or telling her that everything will be okay? Or was she kept in a room by herself, filthy, hungry, and without any human contact? It was enough to bring tears to my eyes.

To make matters worse, a year had passed since my discovery, and I was no closer to finding her. I felt like a monumental failure, like I wasn't trying hard enough. Yet I knew I was doing everything I could think of. In fact, every choice I had made was based on one guiding principle: would doing this bring me closer to finding Mui?

The last year's decisions weighed heavily on me. I would often lay awake at night, questioning myself. Where did I go wrong? Why had I not made more progress? Why had I not made any?

In my profession, I had been tasked with doing the impossible and succeeded. Why could I not do the same for my daughter? Why couldn't all of the skills I'd acquired over my lifetime help me find her? I'd found marks that should never have been found. I'd infiltrated buildings that were impenetrable. I'd done the unthinkable, an unthinkable number of times. Why was finding Mui proving to be the anomaly?

The taxi jerked to a stop and snapped me out of my thoughts. The driver pointed at a building across the street. I wiped my eyes with the back of my hand, paid the fare, and exited the vehicle.

Obstetrics was located in the east wing on the third floor. The overstuffed elevator opened into a crowded waiting room. There wasn't a smiling attendant waiting to answer my questions here. Instead, I faced a line of people and a single nurse helping them. A quick look was all I needed to see that the line was moving at the speed of incompetent-employee-helping-ignorant-customer.

I stopped a passing nurse, but she had a heavy accent, and it was very difficult to understand her. I eventually used up my three requests for her to repeat what she was saying; it had become awkward. We smiled at one another and parted.

I intercepted workers one by one, but they were either too busy to speak to me, didn't speak any English, or if they did speak English, shrugged and said they hadn't heard of her. I could have taken their word, but I needed to be sure. What I wanted was someone to look at a list of employees and tell me that nobody by that name worked there or "Yes, she's here and her shift starts at this time." I needed that level of confirmation to feel satisfied before moving on to the next hospital.

The more passersby I asked, the more conflicting the answers had become. Bumrungrad had led me to believe there was hope in bureaucracy. I should have known better.

I left BNH eighty-percent sure that Amina didn't work there. Samitivej Hospital didn't prove to be any better. In fact, it was worse. Security and a hospital administrator stopped me shortly after my arrival.

"You must make an appointment with the proper administrator," she said, peering at me above her bifocals.

I wasn't sure if she had a stick up her rear or had pulled the bun on her head too tightly. It was probably a combination of both.

"Employees are not allowed to talk to insurance

representatives," she said sternly.

"Can I talk to you?" I asked.

"No."

"Aren't you an administrator?"

"Yes, but you must talk to another administrator."

"Can I talk to this other person now?"

"No. That person is on holiday."

Each response was delivered without that polished Thai smile.

"You give me your card and I will have them call you."

"It's a pressing issue. I don't have the luxury of waiting."

Silence followed, then a customary smile and eventually a hand showing me to the elevator. It was passive-aggressiveness at its finest.

Chapter 61

After I left Samitivej Hospital, I stopped for a bite to eat at a small noodle shop. I choose a small table on the sidewalk, under the awning and away from the other diners. Given that I had spent most of my time in air-conditioned buildings and vehicles, I hadn't fully realized how sweltering the heat was that day. My blouse clung in all the familiar areas. While I waited for my noodles, I hoisted my hair into a makeshift bun using a plastic chopstick, dabbed myself with a napkin, and downed two cups of ice water.

Needless to say, my lack of progress had me frustrated. I could say with certainty that Amina wasn't employed at Bumrungrad; there was a chance she worked at BNH; and as for Samitivej, I might as well have never visited because I got no indication either way. There was a real possibility that multiple trips to the same hospitals would be required for me to be able to cross them off the list. I had to wonder if I'd executed Akil a bit too early. I had always intended to do away with him, but only after I was sure I had what I needed from him.

My mood was that of newbie assassin on her first day of work, relegated to eating alone in the lunchroom.

Nothing seemed to go as planned, and it was taking an inordinate amount of time to get results. But the worst part was that this was perfectly normal in my profession. I'd had contracts where I spent weeks meticulously planning only to have the operation go sideways from the start. But I adapted. I didn't get bogged down with what I thought would happen but instead focused on what needed to be done. There was a goal, and there were many roads leading to it, but in this instance, I didn't want to hear any of that.

Perhaps I was restless that day. Maybe I was too eager to find my daughter. Who could blame me? I had chased a tiny lead Kostas had given me from Paris to Bangkok. And each time I thought it would pay off, it changed course. It was like climbing to the top of a mountain only to realize what had seemed like the summit actually wasn't.

I had just finished my bowl of noodles when Kostas rang my cell. "Please tell me you have good news," I answered.

"You sound a little down. Are you still in Ho Chi Minh?"

"No. I was only there for about twenty-four hours. I'm in Bangkok. And it's hotter than hot."

I brought Kostas up to date on what had happened since my arrival in Vietnam.

"Wait, Akil is dead?"

"Yes. It's unfortunate. He had a terrible accident and impaled himself. Poor thing."

"I have a feeling that accident was premeditated."

"Anyway. Amina Jelassi. Tell me you have something," I said, wanting to move the conversation forward.

"I hate to say it, but I don't. No criminal records, and she's not a person of interest for the CIA or the authorities in France. I gave her name to a contact in Tunisia but honestly, I'm not hopeful. Amina probably lived a straight life and got herself innocently wrapped up in this mess."

"I was afraid that might be the case."

"How's the search coming along?"

"Slow."

"Too bad Akil had an accident. Maybe there was more information to be had."

"He would have had an accident sooner or later."

"Not to rain further on your parade, but how sure are you that he even gave you the right name?"

"I can't be, but I don't think he had any more information to provide, and what he had told me thus far checked out."

"Even if he had given you her real name, she could be using an alias or have a different name on her passport. It's possible if she's on the run."

"I realize that," I said, letting out a breath.

"Did you ever get a look at any of the nurses that day? Amina might look familiar."

"Delacroix was the only person I had contact with

before I was put under. I vaguely remember an anesthesiologist entering my room. At least I assumed that's what she was. She was dressed in scrubs and wearing a mask."

"And after the procedure? Still no interaction with the staff?"

"When I woke, it was late and the clinic had already closed. Only Delacroix was around, and he kept watch over me until I was able to leave. I didn't think it was strange at the time. I had hired Delacroix to perform a very private birth. Interacting with him and only him was what I had always intended. I did hear voices outside my room before giving birth and caught glimpses of staffers outside my door every time Delacroix came in and out of my room."

"Chin up. There's still the possibility that the nurse you saw might be Amina. Plus, in the big scope of things, you know more now than you did a few weeks ago."

"I know that the Wolf is executing everyone connected to the kidnapping. I'm not so sure that's a plus. If he succeeds, it'll only make my search harder."

"Look, I'm keeping my ears to the ground on this Wolf guy. I'm doing what I can."

"Thank you."

There was a pause before Kostas spoke again. "Have you had a chance to sample the Thai cuisine?"

"I just finished a bowl of roast pork with noodles."

"That sounds tasty. If you get a chance, try *yum naem*

kao tod. It's a salad made from fermented pork sausage and mashed-up, deep-fried rice balls, fresh ginger, lime, basil, peanuts, and chili. It's the perfect combination of crunchy, tangy, spicy goodness."

"Great. I wrote it down." I knew Kostas was trying to keep the situation upbeat, but I wasn't in the mood to be handled, let alone coddled.

"You didn't write it down did you?"

"No."

"Well, you should. If you want, I can email you a list of must-have dishes while there."

"*Yum naem…* I'll look for that the next time I feel the need to eat."

"You'll thank me. In the meantime, I'll continue to poke around on Amina. Stay safe, Sei."

I hung up wondering if Akil had really sent me on a wild goose chase. There was no way to know. All I could do was follow through and see if anything came of my search for the nurse.

Chapter 62

My next stop was Sukhumvit Hospital. It was short distance from where I had eaten lunch in Thonglor—a seven-minute ride on a motorbike taxi to be exact.

The hospital was smaller than the others, just a tall singular building with obstetrics located on the fifth floor. I exited the elevator and didn't find the chaos I had experienced at Samitivej Hospital.

It had a modern feel, probably recently built or, at the very least, renovated. Neutral tones graced the walls, furniture, and carpeting. It was quieter as there wasn't much of crowd that day. The staff spoke in hushed tones, and the coolness of the air conditioning was refreshing.

I approached the reception desk for the floor and proceeded to give the attendant my insurance story. Her hands were stacked on one another in front of her, and she had a pleasant smile. She listened attentively, nodding every so often. I couldn't help but think my experience here would be similar to the one I had at Bumrungrad. My spirits were lifted, cautiously.

And then she opened her mouth.

"Sorry, I'm not able to answer that question."

Is she not authorized to give out this information, or did she simply not understand my question? "I just need to know if she's employed here. If the answer is yes, I'll contact the correct administrator to connect with Amina."

"If you don't know if she works here, why did you come here?"

I was beginning to think the woman grasped about twenty percent of what I said. "As I stated earlier, she no longer works at the hospital we have on file, but we know she's still working in Bangkok. We're just not sure which hospital. It's my job to find that hospital so that we can contact her."

She smiled and said nothing.

"Am I making sense?"

She nodded.

"But you're not planning on saying anything, right?"

Her smile widened, and mine retracted.

Plan B was to stop staffers, away from the reception desk. I thanked the lady and asked where the nearest bathroom was located.

"At the end of the hall," she said, pointing.

I headed in that direction until I was out of her sightline and began discreetly intercepting staffers. The first three shook their heads—no, they hadn't heard of that name. The fourth person said it sounded familiar but couldn't be sure. She walked away before I could press her any further. I received two more nos and another yes.

A woman with a stack of manila folders held tightly against her chest approached me. Her eyes were focused on the door leading to the women's restroom. A look of determination covered her face. *I'll catch her on the way out. She'll be more willing to chat then.*

A few minutes later, she exited the restroom with a much more pleasant expression. "Excuse me," I said, quickly reciting my story with a smile.

"Jelassi?" she asked.

"Yes, Amina Jelassi."

She pursed her lips, and her eyes shot up to the left. "Are you sure her name is Amina?"

"It's what I have in my records."

"There is a nurse here whose last name is Jelassi, but her first name isn't Amina. It's Sarra."

I inhaled sharply and straightened up. Could it be? Had I found her? "Oh, maybe Amina is her middle name. She's Tunisian. Has an olive complexion." I had no idea what Amina looked like, but I figured I could get close with her Tunisian background.

"Yes, I think you are talking about Sarra Jelassi, but she's not from Tunisia. I think she mentioned France."

I found her! "Yes, I believe she immigrated to Thailand from France. I think this is the person I'm looking for. Is she working today?"

"I don't think so. I haven't seen her, but that doesn't mean she's not. I'm not a nurse. I work in Patient

Payments."

I glanced at the plastic badge that was clipped to the lapel of her uniform.

"Preya, could you please check and see if she's scheduled to work? Better yet, a home address would be wonderful."

She shook her head, and crinkles formed near the bridge of her nose. "I'm sorry, but I can't give you that information. It's against policy."

I discreetly removed three hundred euros from my pant pocket and placed it in her palm. "It's such a small favor. I just need a home address, and I can visit her there."

She opened her hand enough to see the euros and then looked around to assure herself that nobody had seen me place it there. "You have to come back at nine p.m. when my shift is finished. Just ask for me at reception, and I'll come and meet you."

My smile returned. My heart fluttered. I had finally taken a step closer to finding Amina.

Chapter 63

It was nearly eight p.m. when Amina finished with her day's worth of chores. Even though it was her day off from the hospital, it wasn't a day off from Houda. She had spent the morning cleaning the room and washing four loads of laundry. She then made a trip to the market, ran errands for the family, and spent the remainder of the afternoon babysitting the children while Houda and her husband went to the cinema.

When the lazy couple returned, so did the demands. "Something cold to drink." "I need a foot massage." "Why isn't dinner ready?"

Houda always expected a more substantial dinner on Amina's day off, as she didn't have to work and therefore had more time to prepare. By the time Amina cleaned the dishes and bathed each child, she was worn out. It had been non-stop from the moment she woke at seven that morning.

With all three children busy playing video games on their tablets, Houda consumed by her soap opera on TV, and the husband snoring on the bed, Amina excused herself and headed up to the roof.

Once there, Amina lifted the hem of her shirt and

removed the bottle of peach tea from the waistband of her jeans; she had purchased it while grocery shopping. It was on these days that she really felt the need for her tiny pleasure. Serving the family took everything out of her. She relished her time spent at the hospital, away from them.

Amina took a seat in the spot between the two water reservoirs and savored the first sip. She pulled her hair back into a ponytail and fastened it with a scrunchie. There was a nice breeze that night, which helped to diminish the day's stored heat as it rose from the roof. Even when the wind was absent, she wasn't deterred. Better on a hot roof than in a cold room.

She stared up above and found her favorite constellation, the Southern Cross. A smile formed as her eyes traced the outline. Amina believed locating it every night was an omen for good luck—a sign that she had a better future ahead of her.

Lost in the sparkles above, Amina didn't notice the man right away, not until he moved away from the entranceway to the rooftop. She perked up. Rarely did anyone from the building come up to the roof that late at night. There were no clothes to be collected from the clothesline.

"I'm sorry," the man said. "I didn't mean to disturb you."

"It's okay. I don't own the roof." She peered at the man's face as the moonlight gave it life. He didn't look familiar, so she stood up to leave.

"No, please. Don't leave," he said, motioning for her to remain seated. "The sky is too beautiful and the night still young. And to be honest, it'll be refreshing to chat in English, as my Thai isn't that great. That is, if you don't mind."

He had a gentle smile and dressed nicely, and there wasn't anything threatening about his demeanor. Amina relaxed her posture. "Are you new to the building?"

"I'm thinking about moving here, but I wanted to see the view from the roof, as I like to look at the stars. I find it calms me." He stood a few feet away from her, head craned back as he stared upward. "You share the same interest?" he asked, still looking up.

"I do..." Amina let her words trail briefly before speaking again. "You're not from Bangkok."

"No, I'm not. You mind?" he asked as he eyed an overturned bucket.

"Not at all."

He positioned the bucket next to her and sat. Amina's nose picked up a faint citrus scent, either cologne or deodorant. She couldn't tell.

"I'm originally from Tibilsi, in Georgia," he said. "You heard of this country?"

"I have. It's a long way from here."

The man let out chuckle. "I visited Thailand many years ago and always wanted to come back. An opportunity to live and work here came up, and it was an easy decision for me. You don't look like you're from Thailand either."

"I'm Tunisian. I have a story similar to yours."

"Well, I wish us to both have better lives here."

Amina smiled. "What makes you think I came here for a better life?"

The man inhaled deeply before turning his gaze back to the stars. "Everyone is looking for a better life. You and I have had to look a bit farther."

Chapter 64

I visited two more hospitals out of due diligence before I called it a day. I was sure that I had found Amina and that soon I would have an address for her. When I returned to my room, I thought of calling Kostas for an update but let that thought fade. The heat had worn me out, and the call of my bed was too much to ignore.

When I woke, I took another shower and then changed into jeans, a T-shirt, and trainers. It was eight thirty p.m. when I headed toward Sukhumvit Hospital. It was a fifteen-minute taxi ride, but I wanted to arrive early so as not to miss Preya before she left work.

When I arrived to obstetrics, a different lady sat at the reception desk, which I was thankful for. Having to explain my presence again to the statue that sat there earlier wasn't something I was looking forward to.

"I'm here to see Preya Suttiwong."

The lady behind the desk nodded before picking up the phone and making a call. "Please have a seat," she said after hanging up. "She'll be here soon."

I sat on one of the beige sofas, away from the desk, and waited. A few minutes later, I spotted Preya prancing down the hall. She had a unique walk, very light on her feet, almost as if she were walking on a catwalk. She was beautiful, of course, with her fair skin, pink lips, and perfectly manicured eyebrows. All the women in the hospital kept their hair tied back into a bun. On Preya, doing so only further accented the delicate curve of her neck. She held a smile as she approached, which was hopeful.

"I said to come at nine," she whispered once she reached me. "You're early."

I looked at my watch. It was five minutes to nine. "I'm sorry. I didn't want to miss you."

"You must wait until I'm finished. I'll be back."

For a brief second, I thought I was in Germany.

"Wait," I said as I grabbed her arm gently. "Do you have the information?"

"No, because the person who is helping me told me to come back at nine, when her shift is finished."

"Okay. I'll be here waiting."

It was twenty after nine when Preya returned. The thought had crossed my mind that maybe she wouldn't return. With Akil dead, Amina was my only hope at keeping the lead alive. It created nervousness in me that I hadn't experienced much. It had me expecting the worst: information that wasn't actionable.

Preya handed me a piece of paper. "She lives in On Nut. Do you know where that is?"

"I'm new to Bangkok," I said as I looked at the

address.

"Take the Skytrain to the On Nut station. It's two stops. Very easy. From there you can take a motorbike taxi to Soi 20 on On Nut Road."

Her instructions seemed simple enough, and the name of the apartment complex was MT Living. I didn't think it would be problematic. I stood and thanked Preya. As I was about to leave, she placed a hand on my shoulder, stopping me. A tiny crinkle formed on her forehead.

"There was another person asking for Sarra… I mean, Amina."

In an instant an empty feeling erupted in the pit of my stomach as the joy-high I had been on was sucked from me. "Who?"

"I don't know. The person who gave me her information said another person had asked for her address about thirty minutes ago."

He found her!

Chapter 65

"So, do you like what you see?" Amina asked the man.

"Huh?"

"I thought you were deciding if you wanted to live in the building."

"Oh, yes, yes," he said, nodding. "I think this place will suit my needs. Do many people come up here at night?"

She shook her head. "During the day, they dry their clothes on the lines over there. At night, it's just me. You're the first person I've seen here at this hour."

"That's good to know."

"Why do you say that?" she asked with a tiny chuckle. "You don't like people?"

"When I'm working I don't like people around."

"Oh?" She pulled her chin back. "Now I'm curious. What type of work do you do?"

"I find people."

Her brows dipped. "You mean missing people? Like children who run away from home?"

"The reason why they're missing isn't of importance. Finding them is."

"Are you good at your job?"

"Yes, I am. I've found everyone I was hired to find." The man stretched his legs out in front of him and shifted his weight on the bucket. Amina noticed that he hadn't removed the knapsack from his back.

"I'm impressed. I've never met someone with this type of job. What do they call it in the movies," she said, snapping her fingers, "a private eye?"

"I've been referred to as one."

"Do you also look for bad people, someone who's running from a crime?"

"There have been a few."

"Aren't you afraid of getting hurt?" she asked. "I imagine it can be a dangerous job."

"I'm not the one who gets hurt."

Amina's eyebrows shot up. She screwed the cap back on the empty tea bottle and placed it next to her chair. "Earlier you mentioned that you already have a job here. So are you looking for someone in Bangkok?"

"I am."

"How long does it take you to find people? Days? Months?"

"It depends." The man glanced at his watch. "Let's see. I arrived in Bangkok this morning," the man clucked his tongue a few times, "and it took me about ten hours to find this person."

"You already found them?"

"I believe I have," he said, turning his head toward her.

"What happens now? You return this person?"

"No, no. My employer does not want her back." The smile on his face disappeared, and his eyes faded into two black pits.

"Her?"

"Yes, her. The person I'm looking for is you, Amina Jelassi."

Chapter 66

Amina shot out of her chair with enough force to send the molded plastic piece tumbling backward, but the man was quicker. He caught her right arm above the elbow and yanked her back into his arms. His hand clamped down around her mouth and muffled her cries for help. Short bursts of his hot breath blasted the side of her right cheek as he held her tightly against his body. She tried to wiggle out of his grasp, twisting her body in every direction, but his hold remained firm and secure.

She continued to fight as he dragged her back between the two water reservoirs, lifting her high enough off the roof that the tips of her shoes barely grazed the surface. Kicking at his shins seemed to produce no effect; the blows glanced off of him effortlessly. She attempted to smash her head back into his, but he kept the side of his face pressed tightly against hers.

In the shadows behind the reservoirs, it was pitch black.

"Who are you?" she finally managed, still struggling.

"I'm the assassin sent to end your life." Mdivani clucked his tongue. "It's a shame. Your life here looked promising."

She tried to speak again, but his grip around her diaphragm had tightened. Mdivani loosened it a tad. He was always interested in the dying's last words.

"Why? I did nothing to deserve this," she said between breaths.

"I think you know that's not entirely true. You remember don't you?"

Amina shook her head.

"You helped with the kidnapping of a little baby."

"I didn't know they were going to do that. The doctor—he was responsible."

"You're right, and now he's dead."

"Was that your wife, the one who gave birth? Are you here seeking revenge?"

Mdivani laughed. "You have it all wrong. I've been hired by the man who planned the kidnapping. I'm here to make sure no one ever finds out what happened."

Tears flowed down Amina's cheeks, and her voice cracked when she spoke. "I didn't tell anybody. I won't tell anyone. I promise."

"That's not how this works. I'm not here to ask you to be quiet."

Amina's sobbing grew louder, forcing him to cup his hand around her mouth again. She choked on her breaths. His body heat fueled her own. Her neck became slick with sweat, and the back of her shirt felt damp. She began to tire, her lungs beginning to burn. Her eyes searched for an escape, a way to signal for help. There must be one. She simply couldn't give up. Not now. Not ever.

"Don't worry Amina. Death will not be painful."

Mdivani forced his left arm under her chin and pulled back against her windpipe. Amina felt immense pressure on her throat. She tried hard to inhale but couldn't. Her lungs ached. She grabbed his arm and pulled with all her might but it wouldn't budge. She kicked and kicked. Elbowed and elbowed. Threw her head back as much as she could, trying desperately to connect with his face, to hurt him, to cause him to loosen his grip just enough that she might escape.

And then she felt it: a loosening in the pressure around her neck.

Yes, he's letting go. He's tired. Keep going, Amina.

Her hand lessened its grip on his arm and fell to the side, dangling.

Just fight a little longer, a little harder.

Her kicking turned into one leg jerking straight out.

You're winning, Amina.

Sadly, the euphoria that Amina felt wasn't Mdivani giving up. It was the life leaving her body.

Chapter 67

Amina's family directed me to the rooftop of the building. I found her curled up behind a water reservoir. I almost missed her. From a distance, she looked like a piece of bunched-up tarp, but I always made a habit of poking everything I see. I've found people in the most unlikely places. She wasn't breathing, but her body was still warm. I turned her over onto her back and proceeded to administer CPR.

Thirty chest compressions and two breaths.

Come back to me, Amina. You can do it.

Thirty chest compressions and two breaths.

Don't give up. You've got a life to live.

Thirty chest compressions and two breaths.

Thirty chest compressions… no breath.

After trying to revive her, I removed my hands from her chest and stared at her lifeless body. A feeling of senselessness grew inside of me, weighing my shoulders down. A tear crawled down my left check. Failure seemed to be something I'd begun to excel at.

I wiped my face with my shoulder, a bit ashamed that I couldn't control my emotions. When I was a child, my mentors told me teardrops were signs of weakness. In that moment, I couldn't help but feel just that: weak and defeated. I had continued to fail over and over in the search for my daughter. Another tear fled my eye, then another, until streams traced both cheeks. I couldn't control the sobbing. I had become someone I never expected: a grieving parent.

I placed my hand over Amina's face just below her eyes to try to determine whether she was in fact the one nurse who came into my room, but nothing about her eyes looked familiar. I so badly wanted to ask her questions about Mui. Did she open her eyes? Did she look at you? Did she make a noise? Did she cry? How long did you hold her? What did she smell like?

That night I realized I had never fully grieved the loss of my daughter. I had kept it bottled up inside. Hiding, avoiding what had happened, was my way of dealing. But once I discovered she was alive, hope grew. Slowly, cautiously, I had allowed myself the joy, the happiness of believing that I would find her. But with Amina's death, I was stripped of any hope, again. An intense pain gripped my abdomen and spread throughout my body like a black cancer. I fell to the side, curled up in a ball, and cried.

Amina's family hadn't bothered to come up to the roof with me. When I spoke with them earlier, I sensed no bond between them and Amina. I had no plans on notifying them—having Amina's death tied to me wasn't an interesting proposition. I composed myself and then walked over to the four-foot perimeter wall at the edge of the roof. I peered down at the street below. A single streetlight just to the right of the building shed light on a ten-foot radius. Just beyond the edge of the yellowish circular glow, to the right, where the blend of dark and light mixed, stood a lone figure.

The assassin!

Chapter 68

I raced down the stairs, two at a time, sometimes three, bouncing off the wall at each turn on the landing between floors.

Boom!

Boom!

Boom!

The pounding on the hollow wooden steps echoed in the halls, but I didn't dare slow. Instead, I mustered as much speed as I could, arms pumping and thighs burning to propel me forward. I had every intention of catching that bastard and making him pay for what he had done.

How arrogant he was to stick around to watch the fallout. He knew I would show. He wanted a reaction, to silently mock me. His decision ignited a vengeful fire inside me. Hot air blasted from my nostrils and the skin between my brows bunched tightly. *I'm going to kill you!*

I burst out of the building, nearly shattering the glass door against the wall. I didn't stop running until I reached the streetlight where I last saw him, but he had already disappeared. I had expected he would hide but not leave the area. He was near. He would continue to watch. I knew the type. They fed off the misery of others, relished in their kills, prolonging them if possible.

I slowed my pace and kept to the middle of the one-lane road. There were streetlights every fifty yards or so, but in between, the night thrived. I reached behind and felt along my lower back. The knife I had purchased earlier was still safely tucked in my waistband.

I approached an empty lot on the left. It looked as if it had been cleared for construction of a new apartment building. The edges were lined with small trees and bushes. In the middle there appeared to be a large trash pile, and the shell of a small vehicle rested near it.

I softened my breaths, allowing my ears to pick up even the faintest noise that didn't belong amongst the singing crickets and the soft rustling of the tree leaves. Even though I quieted my breath, there was nothing I could do to mute the drumming inside my chest.

To the right of the road was a three-story dwelling. It looked like it was next on the chopping block: The windows were missing and the six-foot perimeter wall out front was partially demolished, leaving chunks of concrete scattered in front of the building. A large steel container filled with debris blocked a footpath into the parking lot, but with no wall, entry wasn't a problem. I took a few steps closer.

I know you're here.

I peered harder into the dark shadows, well aware of the increased pinching between my brow and the crinkling above them.

Another half-step forward.

Pause.

Listen.

Scan.

Another step.

I stood where the road and the edge of the property met, eyes shifting, peering, and penetrating the dark. But it was my ears that sounded the alarm.

The slight crackle of gravel prompted me to spin just in time to see him running straight at me. I crouched low on both legs and exploded upward just as he reached me, using his momentum and my arms to push him up and over me. Like a rag doll, he spun around over me but still managed to land right side up on all fours. I kicked my right foot out quickly, and it glanced off the side of his head as he pulled back.

I moved in as he stood, catching him square in his face with a knee strike before he could stand fully erect. His head snapped back, and he let out a grunt. As I brought my leg back down, I followed with a downward elbow strike to the crux of his neck and shoulder. He fell to one knee, but then wrapped his arms around my legs.

He pushed forward, looking to take me down, but I shuffled back, avoiding it. I was relentless with multiple elbow strikes to either side of his head. It felt as if I were striking a bowling ball. I worried I didn't have enough force behind each blow, but his grip loosened, and I grabbed the back of his head and forced it down into three consecutive knee strikes.

The last strike buckled his legs, and he fell to his side. Blood smeared his face. His nose had swelled and the same was beginning to happen to his eyes as he struggled back to his feet. I delivered an upward kick to his face. His body fell forward, and he lay motionless, crumpled on the road. He wasn't dead, but I had destroyed him within the span of ninety seconds. I used my foot to flip him over to his back before drawing my blade and straddling his chest.

"Wake up!" I growled an inch from his face. I pressed the blade against his neck.

He didn't move. I nicked his neck with the tip of my knife. His eyelids opened.

"Who are you?" I asked doing my best to control my voice from shaking.

He stared at me briefly before a grin formed on his face. "I'm like you."

"Don't compare yourself to me. It's futile. Tell me your name."

"Anzor Mdivani," he said between coughs.

I had heard of that name, but that was where my knowledge of him ended. "Did the Wolf send you to kill me?"

He let out another coughing fit. "You were never the target. The girl was."

"Why not? Why go through all of this trouble to eliminate these people when he could just target me?"

"I don't know his reasons. Why are you asking me these questions? You know as much as I do that we don't question the job. We simply fulfill it."

"I'm nothing like you. I only deal with those who deserve to die."

"Then pat yourself on the back and enjoy a cookie." Mdivani let out a dismissive breath. "Amina was my mark. It's not personal. You of all people should understand that."

"You sound like a newbie reciting the rules."

He mumbled something I couldn't understand.

"What's that?"

"I said you're as much to blame for her death as am I. Don't you realize you led me right to her?"

"How long have you been following me? Since Paris?"

"How observant."

"But you weren't the assassin that killed Feki and Yesmine at La Cite."

"I was hired to watch you, but my directives changed before I arrived in Vietnam. Your searching is only making it harder for you. We know who the marks are. You don't. It's only a matter of time before they are all found and executed."

"Do you even know why I want to find the Wolf?"

He coughed out a chuckle. "Of course I do. I know about your daughter... I. Simply. Don't. Care."

"The feeling is mutual."

I stood up and walked away, leaving Mdivani on the side of the road with my knife protruding from his throat. He had all but killed my chance to further the lead. It was heartbreaking to feel progress in motion only to have it come to an abrupt halt, but that wasn't the worst of it. Not knowing what information Amina might have had pained me. Could she have led me to the Wolf? Could she have kept my hope alive?

The following day, I left Bangkok beaten but not defeated. Giving up wasn't in my DNA. My search would continue. That was a promise I vowed to keep.

Chapter 69

The Wolf walked through a carpeted corridor that led from his private office to an open sitting area in the rear of the compound. The entire left side of the hall was built out of reinforced glass, allowing him a view of the woods. He had purposely built the reinforced concrete wall around the compound fifty yards out so as not to feel like a caged animal.

Hanging along the left wall were various medieval weapons that he had acquired over the years: a battle-axe, a double-edged long sword, a number of crossbows in various sizes, and a variety of spears and shields. He was fascinated with that age of terror and longed to own a castle with a moat. Currently, the compound suited his needs. It served as military bunker in the past and had long been abandoned when the Wolf discovered it and renovated it to his likings.

The Wolf detoured through the kitchen and grabbed a can of cola from a stainless steel refrigerator. Most of his men were out searching for the list of people who worked at the clinic. Ivanovich was somewhere in the compound; the Wolf could hear his loud baritone voice echoing off the walls. He thought of finding Ivanovich, but the faint sounds of a little girl's voice changed his mind. He continued through a door that led out of the building and into a twenty-foot-by-twenty foot clearing of the forest. Soft grass covered the ground, and a lone tree stump stood just off center.

Mui stood on top of the foot-high stump while swinging her custom-made nunchucks from side to side. She was dressed in a red and white cotton jumpsuit and trainers. Her straight, black, shoulder-length hair swished with each swing. At the moment, the Wolf couldn't help but think how much she looked like her mother.

"Hi-yah!" she shouted with each swing of the padded sticks. A look of determination graced her face. When she noticed the Wolf watching her, she crinkled her brow harder and put more enthusiasm into her moves.

The Wolf finished the last sip of his cola, crumpled the can, and threw it at her.

Clink!

She batted the can away with the nunchucks and then jumped off the stump. She landed with one of the sticks tucked firmly under her arm and the other held straight out in front.

The Wolf clapped his hands as he walked toward her. "Excellent."

She relaxed her pose and then bowed. When she righted herself, a large smile sat on her face. "I'm getting better," she said, her eyelids blinking enthusiastically as she brushed her bangs off to the side.

"Yes, you are."

The Wolf placed his hand behind Mui's head and pulled her toward him.

She wrapped her arms around his hips, unable to reach all the way around, and squeezed. Her cheek was squished, causing her to mumble her words.

"Speak up, Mui."

She pulled her head back, her light brown eyes beaming wide with pride. "I said I'm going to be the best, Papa."

"I believe you. Now, let's work on your strength."

A Note From Ty Hutchinson

Thank you for reading CONTRACT: SICKO. If you're a fan of Sei, spread the word to friends, family, book clubs, and reader groups online. You can also help get the word out by leaving a review. If you do leave one, send me an email with the link. Or if you just want to tell me something, email me anyway. I love hearing from readers. I can be reached at tyhutchinson@tyhutchinson.com

Visit my website to sign up for my Super Secret Newsletter and receive "First Look" content. Be in the know about my future releases and what I'm up to. There will even be opportunities to win free books and whatever else I can think of. Oh, and I promise not to spam you with unnecessary crap or share your email address.

TyHutchinson.com

The Novels of Ty Hutchinson

Sei Assassin Thrillers

Contract: Snatch

Contract: Sicko

Contract: Primo

Abby Kane FBI Thrillers

Corktown

Tenderloin

Russian Hill (CC Trilogy #1)

Lumpini Park (CC Trilogy #2)

Coit Tower (CC Trilogy #3)

Kowloon Bay

Other Thrilling Reads

The Perfect Plan

The St. Petersburg Confession

Made in the USA
Columbia, SC
14 August 2019